MW00958890

# SEAL
# Strong

## Silver SEALS

*New York Times & USA Today Bestseller*

# CAT JOHNSON

Copyright © 2019 Cat Johnson
All rights reserved.
ISBN: 9781791704957

# CHAPTER ONE

*Virginia Beach, VA*

From behind the lenses of his sunglasses, Silas tracked her progress across the parking lot.

All it had taken was one glance and he'd known immediately it was Maggie. No doubt about it.

Even wearing a bulky sweater that hid her curves, she was unmistakable, from the glint of sunlight bouncing off her blonde hair, to the proud stride in her walk.

Then there was that sultry sway of her hips.

That had been what first caught his eye over ten years ago, that damn sexy strut of hers, way back when he'd seen her walking across the bowling alley when he'd been fresh out of BUD/S.

She'd had a pitcher of beer in one hand and an

overflowing platter of chili cheese fries in the other and he'd fallen immediately in love. She'd been perfection already, but after he watched her face light with a smile and heard her tinkling laugh as she joined the table of her girlfriends, he knew—he was going to marry that woman.

He'd done just that a year after meeting her. Made Maggie O'Leary into Maggie Branson, his wife.

Make that his soon-to-be *ex-wife*. He couldn't forget that.

Silas ran one hand over his dark cropped hair before folding his arms across his chest.

Leaning back against the bumper of his truck, he waited. He saw the moment she noticed him there. She slowed for a step, before she continued forward at the same brisk pace as before.

Finally, she was right in front of him.

Too close to ignore him or pretend she didn't see him, she stopped. "Silas."

He tipped his head. "Maggie."

She glanced past his shoulder at the office building before bringing her gaze back to him. "We should get inside so we're not late."

"We're fifteen minutes early," he pointed out.

In fact, they'd never been late anywhere during their life together.

Amazingly, Maggie had proven to be exactly like him when it came to punctuality, living by the credo that if you weren't early, you were late.

They were kindred spirits. Compatible in every

way.

Well, every way except one. Apparently she no longer wanted to be married, in spite of his desire to remain so.

She pressed her lips together and drew in a deep breath that had her chest rising beneath the white knit shirt she wore beneath the unbuttoned oversized cardigan.

It took every bit of restraint he had to not let his gaze drop to those breasts. To not reach for her, pull her close and kiss the ridiculous idea of divorce right out of her head.

"I love you." He tossed the words out as a Hail Mary.

A last ditch effort to stop this insanity. An attempt to get back their life together—or piece back together what was left of it anyway.

With tears in her eyes, she said, "Love isn't the problem. You know that."

"Then why are you doing this?" He shook his head, still at a loss.

"You know why."

He drew in a breath and let it out. "We can try."

"Silas, we *did* try. Counseling. Mediation." She lifted her hand in the air and let it drop in defeat. "I can't do it anymore. I'm done."

Too bad for her he wasn't done. Not yet anyway.

He wasn't a man who gave up easily. He hadn't been when he'd successfully completed BUD/S with a concussion he'd hidden from the medics and he wasn't now.

Some might call him stubborn. They could be right.

Whatever the word for it—determined, stubborn, crazy—he persisted.

"It takes time," he said.

"No." She shook her head.

The move made him angry. He loved her, but not her stubborn streak.

When she shut down like this and refused to listen or even consider what he had to say, it made him want to tear his own hair out.

Ignoring the hypocrisy that he considered his own determination a positive trait, but hers just an annoyance he said, "Maggie—"

He heard the annoyance clearly in his tone.

He breathed in and mentally counted quickly to ten before he continued, "Why can't we work on this? On us?"

"Because I can't look at you without seeing him. His little body in that coffin—" her voice cut off on a sob. Her eyes flashed with accusation. "You should have been here. If you were, he wouldn't be—gone."

Her voice broke on the last word. He knew damn well she'd chosen it because she couldn't say what she really meant—if Silas had been home Jonas wouldn't be *dead*.

Hot angry tears pricked behind his eyes.

Silas shook his head, but on some level he

agreed with her. If he had a normal job, one that kept him in Virginia instead of sending him half way around the world, their son might be alive today.

He couldn't combat both her accusation and his own guilt.

The fight gone out of him, Silas pushed off the truck and stood. "Ready to go in?"

Brushing the tears from her lashes, she nodded.

As she walked ahead, he reached out one arm and almost looped it around her shoulders, out of habit like he'd done countless times before.

He stopped himself just in time and instead shoved his hand into his pocket.

She'd never want to feel his touch again. She loved him, but he knew she hated him too, just as he hated himself.

Their ten years of marriage took less than one hour to dissolve.

There was something incredibly sad that the greatest country in the world made it so easy to completely sever ties from the closest person in your life.

Although perhaps it had been Silas who had made it so easy by not contesting the divorce. He could have dragged out the legal proceedings, probably for years if he'd wanted to by fighting it, but what good would that have done?

Only a madman would want to be with a woman who so clearly wanted him out of her life.

Luckily it was in his power to give Maggie what

she wanted. He'd been out of their house for months. He was now legally out of their marriage too, thanks to a few strokes of a pen.

Now his only goal was to get the fuck out of the country and away from all the memories that haunted him.

Slamming his truck into gear, he peeled out of the parking lot of the lawyer's office and headed to the base.

He needed to speak to his commander.

He'd appreciated that Command had arranged to keep him stateside for the past two years as he and Maggie tried to put their life back together after Jonas died, but that effort was obviously done. He needed to piece himself back together, without her.

Silas strode into the office and found the commander pouring a cup of coffee.

He didn't waste any time or beat around the bush. Before the man even had time to say hello, Silas said, "I want back on the team."

# CHAPTER TWO

*Aleppo, Syria*

Silas climbed down from the vehicle and glanced around the base, taking in the sounds, the smells, the sights.

As the sun set in a haze of oil fire smoke and the dust of destruction, all the visceral memories assaulted him.

He hadn't stepped foot in Syria for two years, but standing here now, it felt as if no time had passed at all.

It was as if he'd never left. Never gotten the news from home that changed his life forever. Never made his way back from Raqqa to the States in a daze of shock and grief.

He'd spent the last two years stateside trying to

clean up the broken pieces of his shattered life. He'd failed.

Sure, those pieces were swept up into a neat pile, but he'd hidden that mess behind a uniform and a schedule so packed it left no time for emotions.

His life was by no means fixed.

Coming back to Syria to join his team was his next best plan—his only plan. His version of super glue, or maybe more like duct tape. Even if it worked to keep him together, he'd never be the same.

There would always be visible cracks. All he could hope for was that they'd be more like hairline fractures and less like the gouging canyon he felt inside him since it had happened.

Looking around him now, he felt right at home. Syria was as shattered and broken as he was. It seemed fitting.

Here the fight raged on, the players unknowing, uncaring, that he'd just lived through the most harrowing period of his life.

If only he could turn back the clock. He'd do it in a heartbeat. He wouldn't have reenlisted.

He'd have left the Navy, his team, everything that had consumed every year of his adult life and stayed in Virginia. Gotten a job as a teacher or a coach or hell, anything that kept him stateside and at home every night.

He would have done as he'd promised that summer and taken leave.

Would have brought Jonas to the pool on base every day and taught him to swim as he said he would.

He wouldn't have had to apologize to Jonas and Maggie when the call came that sent the team to Raqqa that summer.

Wouldn't have had to see the disappointment in their eyes that he couldn't spend those weeks during school break with Jonas. Just the two of them, the two Branson men, on their own, having fun while Maggie worked.

Then he wouldn't have gotten that news or heard that word.

*Drowned.*

The lure of the pool was too tempting for a boy of seven, even if he didn't know how to swim because his Navy SEAL father was too busy to teach him. The guilt was crippling.

"Lieutenant Commander Branson, sir."

The sound of his name being spoken by the lieutenant in front of him brought Silas out of his own head. He was grateful for the reprieve. "Yes, lieutenant."

"Sir." The SEAL who saluted him looked much too young to be a lieutenant. "I'm here to escort you to the commander."

Silas returned the salute and wondered when he'd started to feel so old. Although he had a pretty good idea and it had nothing to do with the gray that had begun to pepper the formerly dark, almost black, hair of his youth.

CAT JOHNSON

The toll the past two years had taken on him felt more like two decades. The proof was in his appearance, his body, his soul . . .

And that was exactly why he was here. To take back his life. Get the train wreck of his existence back on track.

Silas nodded. "Lead the way, lieutenant."

Adrenaline pumping in his veins, pulse pounding in his ears, he strode fast shoulder-to-shoulder with the younger lieutenant next to him, forcing the man to pick up his speed to keep pace.

"How have things been recently? Any activity?" Silas asked with a sideways glance at the younger man by his side.

He would know exactly what Silas was asking without him having to spell it out.

"Active," the lieutenant answered simply.

That's what Silas had figured. No way to avoid a heightened level of activity in this complex multi-sided cluster fuck where there were no clear sides. Where allies acted more like enemies and enemies pretended to be friends.

The US backed the Kurdish Syrian rebels against the Russian-supported Syrian government, as Turkey, the wild card who mistrusted the Russians as much as they did the US, threatened to enter the fray.

All of that while the warring sides' common enemy, ISIS, still managed to maintain a stronghold in the country and make life hell for the civilians caught in their net.

The state of this country truly was hell, but no worse for Silas than being stateside had been. It didn't matter where he was considering his own personal demons lived in his head and accompanied him wherever he went.

But right now, Silas was on his way to meet his commander, so he'd better hide those demons as best he could.

Commander James Talley was no stranger. Silas had worked beneath him in Syria before—before he'd been called back home.

More than that, Commander Talley had been the one to deliver the news.

The man knew everything about Silas, not just what was written in his record, and that was a double-edged sword now that he wanted— needed—a fresh start.

Even with thirteen years in the teams under his belt, after what had happened Silas knew he'd be watched closer than any FNG. The difference was that at least the fucking new guys were starting with a clean slate.

Silas would sell his soul to be given exactly that. It wouldn't be given, so he'd just have to take it.

Everyone would be watching for him to show any signs of weakness that might endanger the team or the mission. His job was to make sure there were none for them to see.

His escort trotted ahead to pull open the door. For better or worse, they'd reached their destination.

Silas steeled his nerve, straightened his spine and strode in with as much strength and confidence as he'd ever had.

He didn't have to fake it. He was determined to kick ass or die trying.

Commander Talley stood and walked around the desk.

Silas saluted his superior before dropping his arm to shake the commander's offered hand. "Commander."

"Silas. It's good to see you back. How are you?"

The inevitable question.

Silas pulled out his standard answer. "I'm fine. Good. Ready to get back to work."

Commander Talley paused a beat, watching Silas, no doubt evaluating him and his answer, before he dipped his head. "Good. We can sure use you around here. Action has been picking up."

"So I heard."

"The fucking Russians are our biggest headache. ISIS, we can fight. That's a ground battle. But the Russian air attacks on civilians in the rebel-held areas—that's a whole other story. But the biggest issue is the condition of the city. Caring for the civilian casualties has become near impossible. They're down to two operating hospitals and a reported thirty doctors. A convoy of trucks carrying aid to rebel-held areas of Aleppo—food, blankets and clothing—was attacked. Twenty killed."

Silas frowned, seeing things were, if possible, even worse than he'd thought. "How are we handling that?"

The commander snorted. "The Russian foreign minister said they're trying to bomb the terrorists and accidentally hitting the rebel-held cities instead. So we try to help the Kurds beat back ISIS as best we can so the damn Russians don't have an excuse to *accidentally* drop bombs on us or the civilians."

It wasn't much of a plan. To him, it felt more like running around with a mop trying to clean up the spill instead of just turning off the water.

But these were touchy diplomatic times.

Short of declaring all out war, the various sides had to play nice and pretend they all didn't have secret self-serving agendas.

The commander slapped Silas on the back. "It's good to have you back."

"Thank you, sir. I'm happy to be back."

*Happy*. Not a word Silas had said, or meant, in a long while.

It wasn't exactly accurate at the moment, but standing there in the commander's office in Syria, about to jump back into his old familiar life, he felt as good as he had in years.

Here he could do some good. Here he might make a difference.

Perhaps he wasn't feeling exactly *good*, but he was definitely less bad.

For now, that was enough.

# CHAPTER THREE

Silas woke sometime before dawn in dark unfamiliar surroundings.

It took a few seconds for him to remember where he was and to realize that he'd actually slept—fallen to sleep and stayed asleep.

No tossing and turning. No mind racing with unwanted thoughts. No nightmares of his panicked child gasping for air as his tiny lungs filled with water.

It might just have been the first good night's sleep he'd had in two years—and it had happened on a six-inch thick mattress on a rocky rack that squeaked when he moved.

Why had he slept peacefully here and now when he hadn't in two years? He should be grateful and not question it, but hell, he did anyway. It must be muscle memory or something akin to it.

His body remembered that here he had to sleep when he had the chance, regardless of the conditions—environmental or emotional.

It had been the right decision to request this assignment.

Taking bereavement leave hadn't helped—too much time with nothing to do but to think.

The stint of administrative desk duty stateside he'd requested in an attempt to make the situation better at home with Maggie had been almost as bad. Recruiting duty wasn't any better.

But now, finally, he was free to do what he wanted. What he needed. And what he needed was to be active.

He needed action. Needed to *do*, not think. To be part of a team. To have a goal that is bigger than just surviving one day at a time.

As he pondered getting up and getting his day started even if it was still early and he could stay in bed, the deafening sound of a siren cut through the pre-dawn air.

Flipping back the blanket, he felt the surge of adrenaline hit his bloodstream. The rush only reinforced his opinion. He was meant to be here. He'd made the right decision.

Silas jumped from bed, his sock-covered feet hitting the cold floor as he reached for his pants.

Finished dressing, he heard the shouts and the pounding sound of the boots of his teammates in the barrack's hall. Reaching for his weapons, he knew he never wanted to do anything else.

He ran into the cool damp air toward the ready room, a few of the other members of the SEAL units on this base beside him. He recognized most, though not all, but this wasn't the time for a reunion anyway.

The commander was there when Silas entered. Talley didn't make them wait to hear what had happened or what their orders would be. Hell, he didn't even wait for every man to arrive.

A few stragglers slipped in as he began, "There's been an air attack. All reports indicate it hit a heavily populated rebel-held area in eastern Aleppo. We're going in to secure the site and help where we can. Expect heavy casualties."

So this was what it had come to. Uncle Sam's most highly trained special operators, who were brought in to advise and assist in the war against ISIS, were instead acting as first responders because the fucking Russians were hitting civilians under the guise of fighting terrorists.

"Move out!" the commander ordered as the room erupted in motion.

As Silas shouldered his way out the door, the lieutenant who'd met him upon his arrival the day before trotted up next to him.

"You're in the vehicle with me, lieutenant commander." He pointed to the Humvee ahead.

Silas nodded and pivoted to follow the man to the vehicle. He'd just hopped into the passenger seat as the LT took the driver seat, when the back doors opened and two more SEALs piled in.

Twisting in his seat, Silas turned to see who'd joined them. He nodded to the two SEALs he recognized but didn't know well. At least not much more than their names. It just reinforced that he'd been gone too long.

Silas hadn't even gotten to the reorientation meeting scheduled for zero-seven-hundred this morning.

No matter. They'd all get to know each other better later. Right now it was time to get back to work.

Silas turned back to face the windshield while the red glow on the horizon grew larger as they traveled toward the bomb zone.

He'd thought the situation in and around Raqqa back in 2014 had been bad when he'd been there with the team battling ISIS, but the biblical level of destruction in Aleppo two years later truly made it feel as if they were descending into the depths of Hell as the vehicle bounced over the rough road.

The sirens, the smoke, the screams . . . Dante himself could have written the scene playing out in front of Silas when they arrived on the outskirts of the area that had been hit hardest.

It was a literal inferno. But unlike Dante's seventh circle of Hell, the demons here used Russian warplanes to drop bombs instead of Hellfire in support of the Assad regime. While on the other front, radicals said their prayers before wielding AK-47s and deploying chemical weapons upon innocent women, children and the elderly.

There were enemies everywhere on the

battleground that this country had become—but Silas knew his worst enemy was inside his own head. That was exactly why he'd come here. To purge his personal demons. Toss out the enemies living in the gray matter between his ears. Or at least bury them all so deeply they'd never find their way out.

The lieutenant slowed the vehicle as he navigated around the rubble and debris—and victims.

Some were crumpled in the street. Others stumbled, dazed and bloody. Looking for shelter. Looking for loved ones. Looking for escape from the inescapable.

"Fuck." The sight had the lieutenant cursing softly beneath his breath.

Silas couldn't agree more as he swept the scene with his gaze.

They approached an obstruction in the road. Their vehicle—and their progress—came to a complete stop.

A truck, flipped on its side, blocked the road ahead.

Silas squinted at the pile of rubble and metal being lit by the vehicles headlights as movement caught his attention.

A glimpse of white fabric. A bit of red. A flash of motion . . .

He leaned forward and the movement happened again.

"There's somebody alive under that truck."

Heart pounding, he reached for the door handle.

Silas was outside the vehicle and running toward the scene before the others could respond to his comment.

Counting on his teammates to cover his six, Silas ignored the chaos around him as he dropped to his knees amid the rock shards near the twisted metal.

A tiny hand and arm were visible and not much more besides the sleeve of a blood and dirt-stained shirt.

Silas was clawing at the debris with his bare hands by the time the others arrived to help. He pawed away enough of the rubble to be able to grasp the wheel well of the truck.

Standing, knees bent, he hooked the fingers of both hands beneath the edge of the metal frame and shouted, "Help me lift it!"

There was barely room to stand. The piled debris formed a mound around the truck that Silas had to straddle just to get a foothold.

To his left, the lieutenant tried to get a hold on the truck but was having trouble.

Silas saw the fingers on the small hand twitch, the movement weaker than before.

There wasn't any time to wait. This was someone's child. Some man's son, just like Jonas.

This child was helpless and alone. Gasping in an attempt to breathe just like Jonas, but drowning in rubble and the blood filling his lungs rather than swimming pool water.

But no. It wasn't like with Jonas, because this time Silas was here.

He couldn't save his own son, but he could save this child. With every ounce of strength he had in him, Silas heaved.

It didn't move.

The angle was wrong. He was standing too far from the body of the truck. It was too hard to get a firm footing.

He kicked at the rubble and managed to get a space cleared big enough for his boots so he could stand on solid ground closer to the truck.

A small group of men surrounded him now. A few tossed rocks to the side, trying to reduce the pile so they could get closer to the vehicle. Some were SEALs, others civilians.

Syrians. Kurds. Americans. It didn't matter who they were or to which side of the conflict they were loyal, they worked together toward a common goal—freeing the child.

Standing as close to the truck as he could get, Silas grasped the chassis again.

To his left, the lieutenant was on the ground with his feet braced against the axel that supported the tire in the air as the truck lay on its side.

On the other side of Silas, a local man had a handhold on the truck's fender.

With a nod to Silas the lieutenant signaled he was ready.

Silas returned the nod and said, "On three. One, two, three!"

With a groan of determination, Silas lifted.

He felt the truck move. Felt something in his back pop. Felt the searing heat slice through him.

Still he held on, keeping the truck off the ground, if even just a few inches as two SEALs scrambled to pull the child out from under it.

Through the tears of pain Silas saw the tiny bloodied and filthy body emerge.

"We got him! He's free."

At the words shouted from behind him, Silas released his hold and then dropped to his knees.

He was draped over a pile of rocks waiting for the pain to subside enough he might be able to stand when a pair of boots came into sight. "Crash? Is that you? Damn, why didn't I know you were back?"

Silas recognized the voice, or more the heavy southern accent, if not the generic boots in front of him.

Brad Carr.

He'd known the SEAL for years. Since long before Silas had been promoted to lieutenant commander, from back right after BUD/S when almost everyone called him Crash.

It seemed Silas still hadn't shaken that damn nickname he'd gotten when he'd had a fender bender with one of the trucks his first year with the teams.

He couldn't quite move to look up at his old teammate, but he managed to answer through teeth clenched in pain. "Got here yesterday."

"Jesus, you a'ight?" Brad asked.

Brad was an old friend but it didn't matter who was asking, stranger or friend, because Silas's answer would have been the same.

"Yeah. Fine. Just pulled something. I'll be okay in a minute." He tilted his head and saw Brad had dropped down into a squat next to him.

"You don't look fine to me." Brad lifted a brow, which Silas could barely see through the blinding pain.

Time to suck it up and stand, no matter how badly it hurt.

If word got around to command he'd blown out his back, they'd yank him off combat duty. He hadn't come all the way to Syria just to be sent home again one day later.

He braced his hands against the pile he'd been leaning on and straightened his arms. He pushed but had no strength. It felt like a hot knife searing through his lower back, sending fingers of pain down into his legs.

Brad's hand under his arm might have been the only thing that got Silas up on his feet.

He struggled to stand. Bent like a ninety-year old man, he tried to straighten. He managed a couple of inches before he gave up.

Finally, he lifted his eyes, if not his head, to glance at Brad.

By the gray light of dawn Silas saw the concern in Brad's expression.

"I think you better get your ass to Medical."

"No, I'm all right." Silas shook his head and

was pleased to see his neck still worked fine.

Just a little lower back issue. Some sports rub, a couple of ibuprofen, maybe a heating pad and he'd be good.

He remembered the cause of all this and pivoted stiffly to look behind him.

"Where's the child?" he asked.

"They put him in the truck. They're fixin' to bring him to the hospital . . . if the hospital's still standing, that is."

One word caught Silas's attention, twisting his heart.

*Him.*

He raised his gaze to meet Brad's. "It was a boy?"

"Yup."

Somebody's son. Just like Jonas.

"But he was alive? Still breathing?" Silas asked.

"Weak but still breathing when I saw him, yeah."

He'd saved him. Thank God.

Letting out a breath of relief, Silas nodded. "Good. Good. Thanks."

Brad widened his stance and crossed his arms over his chest. "You going to admit you're hurting now?"

"I'm not hurt."

"A'ight. Then let's go clear some of them buildings and look for more survivors. Come on." Brad spun on one combat boot and then glanced back, waiting.

Silas took one step, then a second.

Maybe walking would help. He could loosen up the muscles. That would ease the pain and stiffness.

Sure. That could work.

Brad led the way, faster than Silas could follow, to a building with the front wall blown out.

"We gotta clear a path and get inside," Brad said from ahead.

Silas caught up and stepped next to him.

Brad had his hands on a beam that had fallen across the doorway. "Grab the other end of this for me."

He did as asked, hooking his hands beneath the wood.

"On three," Brad said. "One. Two. Three!"

Silas heaved as a groan he couldn't stifle tore from him. He dropped his hold on the beam and collapsed over it.

"Yeah, I thought so. *Fine*, my sweet ass," Brad grumbled. The man never did pull any punches but he was absolutely correct.

In his current condition not only was Silas no help, he was a hindrance to the team. If the shit hit the fan, he would be a danger to the others. His inability to pull his weight—literally—could cost lives.

Silas needed to get back to base.

Fine. He'd go. He'd get an ice pack, or a heating pad, or whatever the hell he was supposed to use to fix whatever he'd done to his back, then he'd be good as new in a couple of days.

Brad leaned down, putting his face right in Silas's view. "So, how's that trip to Medical looking to you now?"

Even though Brad was right, he didn't need to be such a smart ass about it. And it didn't mean Silas wanted to hear it.

Through the pain, he managed to growl out between clenched teeth, "Fuck you, Carr."

Brad grinned as Silas accepted that it was himself, and his back, that were good and truly fucked.

# CHAPTER FOUR

*Home.*

It was a word that had never been far from the forefront of Silas's mind while he was away from it. But being here now felt more like a punishment.

*Irony.*

Now that was a word Silas had never thought much about before, but the meaning of it was sure slapping him in the face now as he pushed the button to open the garage door of his former home.

How many times over the past decade had he been in some hell hole around the world and thought longingly of home, wishing he could be there? He couldn't even begin to count.

Now that he was here, he couldn't be more miserable. Although the building he stood inside now was definitely no longer his home. The divorce had determined that.

*Medical leave.* He let out a huff just at the thought of it. He'd probably be put back on the desk duty he hated so much while he healed.

And how long would healing take? How long before he'd be cleared for combat duty again?

He could only guess at this point and none of his estimates made him happy.

Only an idiot would prefer Aleppo over Virginia Beach. Apparently he'd done some major damage to his brain as well as his back because he really didn't want to be where he was.

He exhaled and saw his breath in the cold winter air as he strode across the garage. He started to slide boxes forward on the shelves to check inside and found that he huffed harder from the exertion.

How sad was it that opening the lids of some cardboard boxes was enough to make him winded?

Though he knew it wasn't the effort, but more the pain that had him breathing heavier. And the fact he was rushing to get in and out, because even though this had been his garage for years, it wasn't any longer.

In and out, quick, silent and invisible—it was the SEAL way. His mind might be thinking like a SEAL but unfortunately his body wasn't cooperating.

He was trying to figure out how to reach the box on the bottom shelf without having to bend to do it when he heard the door between the house and the garage open.

"Silas?"

*Busted.*

He straightened, stifled a groan and turned stiffly to face Maggie. "Hey. Sorry."

He shouldn't have come without calling her first. Hell, he probably shouldn't have come at all, but he needed something.

"What are you doing here?" she asked.

The subtext of that question said he was no longer welcome in what used to be his house.

He pressed his lips together and drew in a breath to quell the resentment. "I needed something I left here."

Her brow furrowed in a frown. "What do you need?"

What the fuck was that look and that question about? Didn't she believe him? Did she think he was some sort of obsessed whacko?

"Look. I'm not stalking you or anything. I'm not trying to get back in your life. I came here on a workday figuring you wouldn't be home and I could get what I came for without ever having to see you. That's why I didn't call. So I wouldn't bother you."

She took the few steps to close the distance between them. Reaching out, she laid her hand on the arm he had braced on the shelving as he tried to remain upright without wincing. "Silas. It's fine. Just tell me what you need and I'll help you find it."

He was ranting like a lunatic for no reason and she was the calm logical one.

When had their roles reversed? He was used to

things between them being the other way around.

At least for the past two years, that's the way it had been. Her hysterical and crying. Him calmly trying to reason with her.

Not anymore. Apparently things had changed. He didn't like change in general. He certainly didn't like this one.

Blowing out a breath, he got back to her question. "I wanted that stretchy thing you bought me that year for Christmas to work out with."

"You mean the one you took out of the box and then never used?" she asked, one brow cocked high.

"Yeah." He averted his gaze in shame.

Okay, so perhaps he hadn't been all that grateful when he'd opened it, and that was rude because she had meant well.

But jeez, he worked out enough with the team. He hadn't needed to add to it at home just because she'd seen this thing on some infomercial.

He pressed his lips together realizing he was stupid to think she'd have hung on to it, especially now after their divorce.

"If you got rid of it already, that's fine. I thought I'd take a look. It used to be out here in the garage."

"I didn't get rid of it. And you're right. It used to be out here, but I've been organizing. It's in a box of stuff in the hall closet. Come on inside. I'll get it for you."

*A box of stuff.* He had a feeling it was filled with *his* stuff.

Feeling bitter, his first thought was that she was

probably gathering it up so she could haul it to the dump or donate it. Cleanse the house and her life of all remnants of their time together, so she could pretend their marriage hadn't happened at all.

And what about Jonas? Was she purging the memories of him along with his childhood possessions?

Scowling, he followed her into the house. They walked through the kitchen and past the entrance to the living room.

He tried not to notice each and every one of the changes she'd made in the house as they walked, but he did anyway.

Gone was the folding metal puzzle table that had always sat in the corner of the living room.

He'd liked to sit and do the mindless task to unwind after a mission. She'd never liked the table in the room. Now she didn't have to put up with it there anymore.

Gone were the pictures of them together too. There used to be half a dozen framed photographs on the mantle, a big eight by ten of their wedding picture among them.

There'd also been one of him and her together in front of their first home after they were married. It had been base housing. That was long before they'd moved and gotten a house out in town.

Now on the mantle stood a bunch of candles instead, surrounding two framed photos that Silas recognized. One was of Jonas laughing as he jumped into a pile of leaves in the yard. The other was of him in front of the Christmas tree surrounded by mounds of gifts and torn wrapping paper.

Silas's heart clenched. Some strange, detached part of his psyche made the comparison and determined that, amazingly, his heartache was more painful than his backache.

"It should be right in here," Maggie said.

She was unaware of his inner turmoil as she continued on to the hall closet by the front door while he still hovered in the living room doorway.

Breaking himself away from the painful memories, he followed her to the closet. As she bent to search, he peered past her to see a cardboard box on the floor beneath the jackets hanging on the wooden rod.

She straightened and turned. In her hand was the big rubber band he'd been looking for. Amazingly, she'd found it.

Maggie handed it to him and then folded her arms. "Is that what you needed?"

"Yeah. That's it. Thanks."

He could see there was something written on the side of the box. He couldn't read what it said. The open flap was in the way.

Curious, he leaned down and felt the stabbing pain in his back. Straightening slowly, if not completely, he switched up his plan.

With one hand braced against the wall for balance, since even that had been affected by his injury, he lifted the cardboard flap with his toe.

Where he expected to see something like *Trash*

or *Donations,* instead he saw his own name written in black marker.

At least she wasn't just tossing his shit in the dumpster. That made him feel moderately better.

"Did you want me to take that? The box?" he asked.

Maggie lifted a shoulder. "You don't have to right now unless you want to. You can wait until I'm done organizing. I was going to just keep throwing anything I found in there as I cleaned."

So she wasn't done with her purge yet. There was still more erasing of their history together to be done. Lovely.

"Quite the cleaning spree you're on. You never did this whole house binge cleaning when we were together," he said, feeling mean.

She shrugged again. "I read that book that came out a couple of years ago. It was about how organization can give you peace and joy, so I thought I'd give it a try."

She kept her eyes averted as she made the explanation sound casual. But what she said, rather than how she said it, captured his attention. She was organizing in an attempt to find joy. Meaning she was unhappy?

Interesting that she wasn't happy either. That made two of them.

"Hmm. Maybe I should read it," he said, attempting to make a bad joke because there was no way in hell organizing his stuff was going to fix what ailed him.

Besides, he had so few things and lived in such a small space now, everything was about as organized as it could get. Short of arranging his underwear by color, there wasn't much more he could do.

She laughed at his suggestion. "Don't read it. You'd hate this book."

Her smile, her laugh, they captured him just as it always had.

How long had it been since he'd seen her smile? Or heard her laugh? He knew the answer to that. Since before they'd lost Jonas.

He wanted to see her smile again. Hear her laugh again. He wanted to be the one to put that expression of joy on her face.

To extend the topic of conversation that amused her, he said, "Eh, I don't know. I like organizing things. I seem to remember you mocking me for separating my screws and nails by size in bins out in the garage. Why do you think I'd hate the book?"

"Because the author talks about how you should fold your socks instead of roll them so that they can relax while they're in the drawer. She says it's their time to rest when they're not on your feet."

"So she's saying my socks need a vacation?" He grinned, enjoying the first light hearted conversation they'd had in years. "I'd think she'd want me to put them someplace nicer than in the drawer then, if she's so worried about their time off. Send them to Hawaii maybe . . ."

Maggie laughed. "See. I told you that you would hate the book."

Her laugh had him smiling, even as he shook his head. "Nah. I might not take it seriously, or do what she suggests, but I couldn't hate something that silly."

The small talk about the sock drawer book having run its course, the smiles and the conversation both died.

She glanced at the thick black rubber band in his hand. "So what inspired you to suddenly want to work out with the resistance band?"

"Is that what it's called?" He glanced down at it. "And here I've been calling it that big rubber band all this time."

She treated him to the lift of one corner of her mouth. Not quite a smile but better than nothing.

"Anyway," Silas continued. "I thought I might do some light exercise in my barracks room instead of having to hit the gym all the time."

Because in his room he could work his injured back in private . . . and cry if the pain got too bad.

Silas had no doubt that with how bad he was feeling right now he wouldn't be able to do anything he used to. He'd have to modify his work out, at best.

Someone at the gym was going to notice and realize how much he hurt. He definitely needed to get himself back up to speed before he went back to working out with the team.

Maggie nodded. "I'm glad you can finally get some use out of it."

"Yeah. And thanks . . . for finding it. And for

giving it to me in the first place."

She let out a short laugh. "Sure. No problem."

Okay, now the conversation, or lack thereof, was starting to feel awkward.

He drew in a breath. He needed to leave before he did something foolish.

"So, you have any plans for dinner? You wanna grab something?"

Something foolish, just like that. *Shit.* Inviting her to dinner? What had he been thinking?

When she opened her mouth to speak, he knew what was going to come out before she said it.

He didn't need to actually hear her say the word *no*. He knew he was a fool for asking just from her expression.

She cringed. "Si. I don't think we should. It will confuse things."

"No, yeah. You're right. We shouldn't confuse things. You know, with the divorce being final and all." He took a step back from her, about to make his escape to end the embarrassment as quickly as possible.

"Hey." She reached out for him, grabbing his hand.

"What?" His gaze moved from where their hands were joined, back up to her face as she dropped her hold on him.

His hand hung loose at his side, missing the warmth of her touch. Missing so much more than just that.

"I'm not saying it'll be like this forever. One day maybe we can get a meal together and be just fine. I just can't do it right now. I can't be your friend. It hurts too much."

So she hurt too. That was comforting, because it would really suck if he were the only one in unbearable pain over their divorce.

Fighting the emotions, he chose to leave on that high note.

He tipped his head in a nod. "Bye, Mags."

Silas stepped around her and headed for the front door. He needed to get out of here and back to the privacy of his barracks room.

Might as well start working on his rehab now. His injury would take his mind off the pain in his heart.

Get fixed. Get back to the team. Get Maggie off his mind.

His To Do list was short but he had a bad feeling the time to complete it was going to be long.

In fact, he might never manage that last part.

# CHAPTER FIVE

"Lieutenant Commander Branson, how are you feeling?" the doctor asked as she entered the room and sat behind her desk.

"Fine. Good. Good as new." Lying came easy. Sitting, not so much.

Silas remained standing on the other side of the desk, feet shoulder length apart, back ramrod straight.

This was the woman who would decide if he kept his career or not. And if he was put back on active duty or was forced out on medical retirement.

He'd been back in Virginia for four months. A third of a year's worth of painkillers, muscle relaxers, physical therapy, and being hooked to electrodes as they shocked his muscles . . .

The calendar and the budding trees and flowers showed it was spring of a new year.

Time was marching rapidly on. He should be completely better by now. Both his back and his heartache.

He estimated himself at ninety-percent healed as far as his injury and ten-percent healed on the Maggie front. Hell, he hadn't even come up with an excuse to call or text her for the past three weeks. That was progress.

If he added the two estimates of his recovery together he was at one hundred percent. Good enough. Time to get back to the team.

Today he'd been summoned by the doctor, he assumed because she too thought he should be healed after all this time. It was why he was being evaluated, so he could go off light duty and back to the team. And dammit, he'd do anything he could to make sure that happened.

The truth was he was better than he had been. He felt good. He just wasn't great. At least not back to normal the way he had been before Aleppo.

But he'd heal . . . in time. And when he did, he'd be good as new. He knew it. Knew his strength. Knew his body. Knew his determination would make up for any shortcomings in the rest.

The doctor however, couldn't know any of that.

How many patients did she see in a day? Dozens? More?

To her he was just a name on a chart with a

blank line waiting to be filled out with *return to duty* or *medical retirement*.

Nope. He wasn't going to let that happen.

His last MRI had come back clean. She had no way of knowing or proving the existence of the residual aches he endured daily and he intended to keep it that way.

"Good," she said. "No pain?"

"No," he answered. "None."

It was almost true.

Flat on the floor rather than the bed he could get a few hours sleep a night without pain keeping him awake.

His strength was back and he was quick and sharp—both in his mind and in his shooting. He'd tested that at the range just yesterday.

Her brow rose and he started to worry she doubted him. "Really?"

"Yes, ma'am."

"That's excellent. Wonderful to hear. I see no reason to not clear you to return to full duty."

*That* was what was wonderful to hear.

He smiled. "Thank you, ma'am."

Silas left the office with the golden ticket to return to his team clutched in one hand as he strode to his truck.

That was another source of contention between him and his residual backache. Driving. But he'd willingly endure it because he was about to get what he wanted.

He ignored the nagging thought at the back of his mind. The one that questioned that if his three-year old Ford with its cruise control and heated seats aggravated his injury, what the hell was a Humvee going to feel like bouncing along the blown out roads of a war zone? He supposed he was going to find out.

Making a plan in his head, Silas tucked the paperwork into the visor and climbed into the truck, happy to see the movement seemed easier each day.

Yup. He was definitely on the mend.

Happy, he went back to his plan.

First, a quick stop by the commissary to grab more ibuprofen for the ever present but dull discomfort in his back. Also, antacids for the ache that all the ibuprofen caused in his gut.

Then he'd head to command and tell them he'd been cleared for full duty. The team had returned from Aleppo while he'd been recuperating. His goal was to be with them the next time they were sent out again.

He slowed the truck, looking for a parking spot. He found one and parked, wishing his body felt as amazing as his mood after getting his clearance.

His mood was so high, he felt like he could sprint into command. He settled for walking instead.

"Haynes. Hey." Silas grinned in greeting when he saw the team leader walking toward him.

"Hey, yourself. You back?" Master Chief Peter Haynes asked.

"I'm back." Silas smiled and held up his paperwork. "At least the doc says I am. Still have to run it by command."

"Good." Pete nodded. "Just in time."

"In time for what?" Silas asked.

"We got us a big, high profile training tonight."

He resisted the urge to groan. After being sidelined for what felt like forever, a training wasn't what he'd been hoping for. But maybe it would be good. It would ease him back into things.

"What time?" Silas asked.

"Twenty-one hundred hours."

He had more questions but decided they could wait until he knew if he'd be there for it or not. "All right. Good to go. Let me get this to the commander. Hopefully I'll see you there tonight."

Pete nodded. "Good luck."

"Thanks."

Pete headed out, while Silas turned to go into the commander's office. He was one step closer to getting back to normal. He couldn't wait.

The commander was seated at his desk when Silas arrived in the office.

"Sir."

"Branson. How are you feeling?"

"Completely healed, sir. One hundred percent. The doctor's cleared me."

Commander Talley cocked one brow high and Silas began to worry. The doc might have cleared him, but it would take the commander to put him back where he wanted to be.

"Not one hundred and ten percent?" The commander asked.

Silas knew exactly what Talley was insinuating. Good wasn't good enough in the teams. They had to excel in everything they did or it cost lives.

"It's hard to judge while on light duty," Silas responded with the truth.

He needed to be challenged in a real world situation to see how his back would hold up. The gym was one thing. Combat was entirely different.

"Then it's lucky for you that we have a training exercise scheduled for tonight."

Silas nodded. "Yes, sir. I saw the master chief in the hall."

"You run through that exercise and prove you're back in the shape you were before the injury and I'll put you back on the team.

It was exactly what he'd wanted . . . so why was Silas so worried?

# CHAPTER SIX

Silas had run through this kind of training scenario countless times. During his training to become a SEAL. In the years since. He'd never thought twice about it.

Today, he second-guessed himself at literally every turn.

If he didn't know that this training had already been planned before he showed up with his letter from the doctor he might suspect command had set it up just to test him, because it sure as hell was testing him. His mind, his will, and definitely his body.

But he knew it had been just a coincidence that they happened to already have a training scheduled.

He'd been working out at the gym like a madman the past three weeks, as much to prove to himself he could as to the others there alongside him. But there were differences tonight that made it painfully obvious he wasn't completely healed.

The weight of the helmet with the night vision goggles attached seemed to increase the ache in his back. His tactical vest with the ballistic plates only added to the burden he carried and the strain on his back muscles and spine.

He should have considered all that long ago. He should have been running twice a day in full kit to get his body used to wearing the gear again and to strengthen his lower back muscles enough to support the added weight.

Hell, he should have hit the obstacle course and really tested his body.

The work with the barbells and gym machines had done shit.

Who cared if he was back to bench-pressing what he'd been before the injury?

It was nothing compared to what he was asking of his body now as he hung from a rope and tried to haul himself up the hull of a ship while in full gear soaking wet.

For a SEAL in full kit, what he wore and carried was already heavy on its own. But it had absorbed double its weight in water after Silas submerged underwater to swim to the side of the ship.

In this Naval Special Warfare version of war games, the high value civilian hostage was being held by the pretend kidnappers on the deck of a beast of a naval war ship.

The ship was docked in Norfolk for repairs and made the perfect site for the mock rescue. But this practice scenario could easily be reality anywhere in the world.

Before the back injury, climbing the ladder lowered to him from above wouldn't have been a problem. He would have been able to scramble up the hull of the ship and board without a second thought. But tonight, with his injury still bothering him, it wasn't so easy.

He felt weak. Yes, his arms were strong. No doubt about it. But he couldn't just depend on his upper body strength during an op like this.

His core muscles, even though he worked them as hard as he dared, couldn't make up for the fact the damage to his back hadn't completely healed.

His range of motion was shot. Twisting and turning while hauling himself up onto the ladder and then up the side of the ship caused enough pain to have him clenching his jaw until his teeth ached.

As Silas finally made it up and over the rail through sheer force of will, he flopped onto the deck, panting, his muscles shaking.

His teammate there shot him a glance Silas saw clearly through his night vision goggles.

His weakness hadn't gone unnoticed.

A team was only as strong as its weakest member and that weak link was glaringly and obviously Silas.

This was just a practice exercise, and not even a live fire one at that, given their public location. But if it had been a real mission and they'd been in a deadly situation, him not being one hundred percent could have endangered both the operation and the team.

His hubris in thinking he could overcome his injury and return to combat duty instead of being honest with the doctor and his commander could have cost lives.

With that sobering realization in the forefront of his mind, Silas got through the rest of the exercise. Mostly because his teammates pulled their own weight plus they made up for any of his shortcomings. But he couldn't let it happen again.

The commander was on site with a few men in suits Silas didn't recognize.

Apparently this wasn't just any old training. They'd been showing off for someone. God only knew whom. Probably some politician.

It didn't matter. With the commander present on the dock when the team came off the ship after the successful rescue of the pretend hostage there was no excuse for Silas to delay.

"Sir, I hate to interrupt but I need to discuss something with you. In private."

Commander Talley drew his brows low. "Now?"

"No, sir. It can wait until morning."

The commander nodded. "All right. I'll see you in my office at zero-eight-hundred."

"Yes, sir. Thank you."

It didn't matter that Silas didn't climb into his

rack until a few hours before sunrise. He didn't care that he had just a handful of hours to sleep before he needed to get up, don a uniform and stand before his commander.

He wouldn't have slept even if he'd had the time.

His mind tortured him as effectively as any insurgent could have, keeping him awake, tossing and turning all night.

He arrived at the commander's office on time and in uniform. Ten minutes early actually. But now that he was there, he wanted to be anywhere else.

Even so, there was no getting around what he knew he had to do.

Silas steeled his nerve and strode into the office.

The commander was standing, coffee mug in hand. He moved around his desk, set the mug down and flopped back into his chair. "So, what is so important that you needed to see me now and didn't take the extra hour of sleep I allowed the team?"

Silas swallowed and said past the tightness in his throat, "I need to stand down."

Talley was silent for a second. "Because?"

It was a fair question.

Silas had been away from combat duty for well over two years between Jonas's death and his injury. The commander was justified in wondering which of Silas's issues was going to keep him out of the action now.

"I'm no longer confident in my abilities. I'm afraid I'll be a detriment to the team. I felt it last night during the exercise."

Commander Talley nodded. "You came back too soon. We can put you in a training position for a few more months. Or as long as it takes until you're healed."

"No, sir. I'm not sure I'll ever be back in fighting shape."

It was the hardest thing he'd ever have to admit to his commander and to himself, that even if his back did eventually heal completely, his mind might not.

He'd lost his confidence in his body and himself. That was death for a SEAL's career.

And as for the commander's offer of a training position, or even recruiting or desk duty—he'd been there already. The only way he'd survived it was knowing it was temporary and that he'd be back in the thick of things soon.

The commander pinned him with his gaze. "Good instructors are critical to the future of the teams."

"I know and I'm not knocking the position. It's just not for me." Silas shook his head. "I'm all in or all out."

His body had already made the decision which one it was going to be.

Silent for a few long moments, the commander pressed his lips tight.

Finally he drew in a breath through his nose and said, "All right. I hate to see you go, but I understand. You start the paperwork. I'll push it through. You'll be a civilian before you know it."

Silas nodded. "Thank you, sir."

Getting what he wanted had never felt so devastating.

# CHAPTER SEVEN

"Hey."

Just when he thought he couldn't feel any lower, that achingly familiar voice behind him had Silas tensing.

This restaurant had been their favorite place to come when they'd been married. He should have known there'd be a risk he could run into her here.

Drawing in a bracing breath, he turned his head and saw her. Maggie.

"Hey," he said for lack of anything better.

Her brows drew low in a frown. "I thought the team deployed. Are you on leave?"

She was still friendly with the other guys' wives. It made sense she'd know when the team left town.

What didn't make sense is that she cared what

he did any longer. Her responsibility for his welfare had ended with his signature on the divorce papers.

His beer braced between his two hands as he faced the bar again, he snorted. "Yup. Permanent leave."

"What?" Her voice rose high with surprise.

Silas sighed and turned to face her fully. As much as he didn't want to have this conversation at all, and especially not with the woman who'd caused the gaping hole that still existed in his heart, he had to answer her.

"I've been medically retired."

"What happened?" Her eyes widened as she visibly swept his body with her gaze.

If she was looking for bullet holes or missing limbs, she wouldn't find any.

"I blew out my back."

She hissed in a breath. "Si, I'm so sorry."

He believed her. It still didn't help. "Yeah. Me too."

"Um, I was just going to grab my take-out order. Nothing much. Just pizza and a salad. If you wanted to come back to the house and join me . . ."

He lifted a brow. Was this a pity date? With his ex-wife? Lovely.

But right now, he didn't care.

He realized he hadn't bothered to eat all day and the thought of pizza, combined with the aroma of it cooking that constantly permeated the air of the restaurant, brought his hunger to the forefront.

Besides that, the dead last thing he wanted to do was go back to the studio apartment he rented in town since he no longer qualified for housing on base.

After fourteen years in the Navy, now that he'd been medically retired all he felt was jobless and homeless.

At least he had his retirement and disability pay. Might as well spend some of it on something he'd enjoy. Drinking.

"You have any beer in the house?" he asked.

She cringed. "No. Sorry."

"No worries." He lifted one hand and signaled the bartender. "Can I get a six-pack of longnecks to go? And then you can close out my tab."

"Sure thing, boss."

*Boss*. Not even close.

He'd been a lieutenant commander in one of the finest, most highly trained elite fighting forces in the US military. But he could imagine himself slipping into a new role—that of sad broken drunk slumped over a bar.

And now he was going to hang out with his ex-wife. His pity party was complete.

Half an hour later he realized pizza to fill the empty hole in his gut and lots of beer to numb his mind actually helped a bit.

So did stretching out in his old easy chair in the living room, amazingly enough.

He thought it would hurt like hell being back inside this house, but the familiar surroundings soothed him. Even if it wasn't his living room any longer, it was sure as hell better than that cold depressing room he was renting.

Christ, his life sucked.

He glanced up and found Maggie watching him.

"You okay?" she asked.

He lifted one shoulder. "I just miss it."

"See, I don't understand that."

"What don't you understand?" he asked.

"How you can miss it. The horrors that you saw. That you faced. I don't understand it. Maybe I never will." She visibly gave up with the flick of her wrist.

Her being so quick to abandon trying to understand made him want to explain.

"War and everything that comes with it—all of that, everything you mentioned—is horrible. No doubt. But it's an excellent teacher. It made me a better man. I've never been sharper or in better shape than when I was active duty. But more, wading through all that destruction taught me appreciation for everything else in life."

A man could only appreciate what he had once he'd seen what it looked like to have nothing.

Maybe that's why he so desperately had wanted to go back. More than the camaraderie and the distraction, maybe he needed to see that even with as low as he'd fallen after the loss of his son and the break-up of his marriage, he still had more to be thankful for than every one of those people he'd seen in Aleppo. Right now he needed the reminder that things could be worse.

In the teams he felt like he had a purpose. Here all he felt was . . . lost.

She nodded, giving him hope that maybe she might get it, just a little bit. Though why he cared any longer if she understood him or not, he didn't know.

"So, what now?" she asked.

He let out a short laugh. "Now, I finish this six-pack and then call an Uber."

She rolled her eyes. "I meant for work."

This topic was far too serious for him, but he knew he couldn't get away with not answering. He lifted a shoulder and opted for the truth. "I honestly don't know."

He could probably survive on his retirement pay alone.

It wouldn't be a great life. He wouldn't be living extravagantly, but he could cover the necessities like rent and food.

What more did he really need?

The fact Maggie made double at her job what he'd earned in the Navy meant she hadn't asked for spousal support in the divorce, so that wasn't a financial issue for him.

He'd never wanted much in the way of material things. His truck had been his biggest and pretty much his only indulgence for himself.

The one thing he really wanted most didn't cost a cent. Peace. In his mind. In his soul.

That was also the one thing he couldn't attain no matter how hard he tried, or how much he had.

Money aside, he needed to get a job if only to occupy his mind. All this time for thinking was going to kill him for sure.

"What if I got you an interview?" Maggie said.

His brows shot high. "An interview where? To do what?"

"Where do you think? DHS, of course. Remember, where I work?" She smirked.

Maybe he was running a little slow from the beer but there were too many reasons why what she said made no sense.

First and foremost, he wasn't a politician, or a man who liked sitting at a desk for a living, and that was who mainly filled the ranks of the Department of Homeland Security as far as he knew.

Second, why would the woman who had gone to such great lengths to end their marriage and get him out of her life, try to get him a job working where she worked?

"That's crazy." If his frown didn't tell her what he thought of her idea, his words hopefully would.

"No, it's not. Why would you say that?"

"You work for the Office of Public Affairs," he pointed out, not seeing the connection or the point of this whole discussion.

What the hell could he do for them?

He could lead a team of warriors. He could follow orders from his superiors, but he wasn't exactly a *people person*. Especially not at the moment while he wallowed in this retirement-induced depression.

"I work as a liaison to the Navy Special Warfare Command for the Office of Public Affairs for the Department of Homeland Security, so don't act like there is no connection between what you used to do and what I still do. But what I was thinking—if you'd open your mind for a second and consider it—is that my boss has connections with all the agency heads. You could easily be a valuable addition to any number of the agencies. You have experience in a lot of the areas DHS works within."

"Oh, really? And what areas are those?" he asked, with a good bit of attitude.

Close quarters battle? Sharpshooting? Basic underwater demolition? *Those* were his areas of expertise and he was pretty sure they'd have zero value to DHS.

She folded her arms, visibly challenging him. "Do you even know all the different agencies DHS oversees?"

"Yes."

She cocked a brow high, obviously not believing him.

"I have a basic idea," he added.

Okay, maybe he didn't know quite as much about the intricacies of the agencies that were a part of the Department of Homeland Security as he let on, but he wasn't going to admit that to her.

He could Google it later and find out.

Mostly he figured DHS fit in somewhere along

with the other governmental departments and agencies. No matter what their official purpose, the end result was usually to make his job in the teams harder.

"You know, you used to come home and complain about how this or that person, or agency or department or whatever, didn't get it. How they couldn't get it because they'd never been where you've been or seen the things you saw." Maggie pinned him with a stare.

He couldn't deny the truth of her words. "And?"

"Don't you want an opportunity to change things?"

The dare was clear in her question. She was baiting him. Knowing he usually couldn't resist a challenge.

He let out a snort. "Is this some kind of '*the best way to make change is from within*' speech?"

She smiled. "Yes. Is it working?"

His lips twitched. "Maybe." Silas shook his head. "But it doesn't matter anyway because there is no way in hell they'd hire me."

Maggie cocked a brow high. "We'll see."

Her confidence stirred something inside him. Something he wished would stay sleeping. A warmth in his cold hard heart. A glow of an ember that with a little encouragement could easily flame up into a full blown inferno.

*Fuck.*

The dead last thing he needed right now was to feel the warm and fuzzies toward his ex-wife.

Time to go. Taking out his cell, he opened the ride share app and requested a car. It said one was two minutes away. Perfect.

"I'm going to head out." He planted his hands on the arms of the chair and hoisted himself up.

He'd always been a little too comfortable in that chair. He'd fallen asleep there more times than he could count.

In fact, everything felt a little too comfortable here. A little too inviting. A little too much like he wanted to stay and since he couldn't do that it was clearly past time he leave.

She rose too from her seat on the sofa. "You driving?"

"Nope. I ordered a car. The truck's parked on the street. I'll come back and grab it in the morning."

Either before she was awake, or after she'd already left for work so he didn't run the risk of seeing her again.

He'd spent too much time with her today. It had felt too good to be here with her. He was going to need to wean himself off her all over again.

"That's fine." She walked with him to the door.

"Thanks for dinner," he said when they arrived.

"Sure." She nodded.

"All right. Bye." Out of small talk, he was about to reach for the knob when she leaned in and wrapped her arms around him.

He stiffened, not sure what to do. The only thing he could think of was to hug her back.

Holding her felt all too familiar. Too good. And too damn painful.

He pulled back and disengaged himself from her unexpected embrace.

"Gotta go." He turned and yanked on the doorknob, before realizing it was locked.

He struggled to flip the lock and get the door open, desperate to get outside where he might be able to breathe again. Maybe then he'd remember she wasn't his to hold anymore.

That whole *to have and to hold from this day forward until death do us part* business was over, in spite of the fact they were both still very much alive. Of course, it still felt as if he'd died inside. Maybe *that* was what that sentiment meant.

When he finally conquered the lock, he pulled the door open wide.

"I'll be in touch about the job interview so we can set up a time for you to go in," Maggie said as he walked through the open door.

Him, getting hired by DHS . . . That was never going to happen.

Glancing back, he snorted out a laugh. "Yeah, okay."

"I'm serious."

"Okay," he said, more sincerely this time.

Let her try if it made her happy, but he wasn't going to get his hopes up. He knew better than to hope for anything anymore.

# CHAPTER EIGHT

"Lieutenant Commander Branson. It's a pleasure to meet you. Thanks for driving in to speak with me today." A man named Chavez, who was apparently a big wig at DHS, motioned to the chair in front of the big desk. "Please, sit."

"Thank you, sir. And please, call me Silas." He didn't have any desire to be addressed by a rank that did nothing but remind him he was now a civilian.

Maggie had done it. Pulled off a freaking miracle. And now he had to hold up his half of the bargain and not embarrass her by blowing this interview, even if he didn't want this damn desk job in Washington, D.C..

He still couldn't comprehend that he was seated across from the director of the Office of Operations Coordination in an interview for a position at the Department of Homeland Security.

From the freaking suit he'd had to buy because it didn't feel right wearing his uniform, to his leaving his apartment before dawn to drive to Washington, D.C., to the fact he was even granted an interview to begin with—it was all too surreal.

Christ, he was going to have to move if, by some stretch of the imagination, he got hired and had to start working here, because a three hour commute, each way, without traffic, wasn't a battle he wanted to fight on a daily basis.

"So tell me, Silas, what made you interested in a position here," Director Chavez asked.

The answer to that question was that he *wasn't* interested in a position there. A nine-to-five desk job—he honestly couldn't imagine anything worse.

Maybe he should apply at a sporting goods store or something. At least then he'd be moving around, up on his feet, and he could play with all the knives and bows and hunting rifles.

Yeah, that's what he'd do. Just a nice part-time job, a few days a week to get him out of the apartment so he didn't lose his mind.

Happy with that plan, Silas turned his attention back to the interview he had to get through before he could get the hell out of there and go find something to eat. He'd been awake and driving for hours and he was starving.

But he still needed to answer Chavez's question and probably many more, before this interview would be over. Time to get creative.

Short and sweet seemed to be the way to go. "Well, sir, I recently left the Navy."

"Yes. I see that." The director referred to the paper in his hand. "Quite an impressive resumé you've got. And even more impressive are the letters of recommendation."

Baffled, he said, "Uh. Thank you, sir."

What letters of recommendation? Silas hadn't asked anyone for those.

*Maggie.*

She must have gotten them. She was a friend of his commander's wife. They took yoga classes or something together. That had to be it.

Christ, how pitiful was it that his ex-wife had to jump through hoops and call in favors from every part of her life to get him a job because he was now too useless to be an active duty SEAL any longer.

If Silas wasn't deeply depressed before, he was now.

The man raised his gaze from the paper and back to Silas. "I think a man with your experience would be of huge value to our agency."

"You do?" he asked, sounding as shocked as he felt.

And what exactly did this agency do?

Silas probably should have researched that. That he didn't was proof he hadn't taken this interview at all seriously.

It was also proof of how much his life had changed because while in the teams he never would have gone anywhere without knowing every detail.

Preparation was the key to success, in the teams and in life.

Obviously he hadn't wanted or expected success here today. All he'd done to prepare was punch the address into his GPS and decide which route would have the least amount of traffic.

The director smiled. "I do. What is your availability?"

"Availability for what, sir?" he asked.

For another interview with another director maybe? Shit, that meant he'd have to make this drive again.

"To begin your employment. I'm assuming you'll need to find a rental locally for during the week. A lot of our staff have apartments in the capital region for the work week, then travel to be with their families on weekends."

Silas cocked his head. Chavez must not know about the divorce.

Maggie didn't work out of the headquarters or for this particular agency. And since she had, for now, kept his last name, Silas supposed there was no reason for the man to think they weren't still married.

Especially since she'd apparently pulled quite a few strings at DHS to get him this interview. That's not something exes tended to do for each other.

If, by some stretch of the imagination, he was going to make a second career for himself at DHS working under this man, he had to be open and honest.

Silas cleared his throat. "Um, well, my wife and I recently divorced and . . ." This part was going to hurt like hell to voice aloud. "We don't have any children. So traveling home each weekend won't be a concern. But just so I'm clear, you're saying I'm hired?" Silas asked.

Chavez nodded. "The position is yours, if you want it."

"Oh." Silas frowned, taken off guard by what he never expected to happen—getting hired for a position he wasn't sure he wanted. "I, uh, don't have to have a second interview? Or, meet with someone else at DHS first?"

Chavez let out a short laugh. "No. Unbelievable, perhaps, given the amount of red tape that usually exists in all levels of government, but the Secretary actually trusts me to make the hiring decisions for positions within my agency."

Silas swallowed. "And what exactly would my position be?"

Best find out what he'd be agreeing to in case he did accept this surreal job offer.

"Strategic Operations and Planning Officer."

His eyebrows rose. "Wow. That's quite a title."

It was certainly a mouthful and sounded pretty damn important. If only he knew what it entailed.

Chavez smiled. "It is overly wordy, I'll admit. But your responsibilities would be pretty straightforward. You'd monitor the information gathered by the intelligence side and the law enforcement side of our office and coordinate response activities accordingly."

"Oh." Silas nodded. "Okay."

Jesus, was he even qualified to do all that?

"Does that mean you accept?" Chavez asked.

Silas let out a short laugh. If they really wanted him, why not?

He was quick to learn and could think on his feet. The SEALs had certainly honed that skill in him. And Chavez must think he was a good candidate for the position or he wouldn't have made the offer.

What the hell. He'd give it a try. He'd done crazier things in his life.

Feeling a confidence he probably had no right to, Silas said, "Yes, sir. I accept."

"Happy to have you on board, Silas." Chavez smiled as he stood and extended his hand.

Silas stood as well and reached across the desk. He returned the smile while pumping the director's hand. "Happy to be here, sir."

The shock of it was, for the first time in a while, Silas actually was. Happy.

# CHAPTER NINE

The moment Silas's ass hit the seat inside his truck in the parking lot he had his cell phone's browser open and was punching *Department of Homeland Security* into the search field.

Yeah, he should have done this last week when the interview was first scheduled. No, he hadn't bothered. Yes, he was ashamed of that fact.

Moving on, he read the search results on the screen, hitting one to expand it.

*The Department of Homeland Security works in the civilian sphere to protect the United States within, at, and outside its borders.*

Hmm. Not a whole lot different than what he'd done with the military.

Next he punched in DHS Office of Operations Coordination. He skimmed the very long description that came up.

Words and phrases on the screen stood out from among the rest and caught his eye. Words that told him what he'd be dealing with, such as *classified information*, *situational awareness* and *response activities*, and whom he'd be working with, like *private sector critical infrastructure operators* and *international partners*.

Maybe this position wouldn't be so foreign to him.

Maggie wasn't crazy for putting him in for it. What the agency dealt with—evaluating, planning and coordinating to protect against threats—was right in Silas's wheelhouse.

He drove away from the parking lot in a daze.

It took him until he was on the highway and headed back to Virginia to fully wrap his head around it.

He had a job. He had no idea what exactly he'd be doing or what his hours were but he had a pretty impressive job title and an appointment with the human resources department in two weeks. He also had a week of training scheduled for right after his intake meeting.

What he didn't already know, he'd learn then, he supposed.

A smile bowed his lips as a bubble of excitement grew inside.

Being trapped behind the steering wheel of the truck for the next three hours was going to kill him. He needed to tell somebody. Share the good news.

The one person who came to mind, the one person he should tell because she'd made it all happen, was Maggie.

It was just common courtesy to call her since she'd arranged for the interview. She was probably wondering what had happened.

Happy with that sound reasoning for calling his ex-wife, Silas hit her name in his contacts list and put the cell on speakerphone as it rang.

When the ringing stopped, her sweet voice filled the truck as she said, "Silas. Hi. How did it go?"

He didn't make her wait for an answer as he smiled. "I got the job."

"Oh my God! You did?"

"Yup. I'm not exactly sure what the job is." He chuckled. "But I figure whatever it is, I'll find out soon enough. I start in two weeks."

"Holy cow. That's wonderful. I'm so happy for you. But two weeks isn't all that long. You're going to look for a place to live closer, right?"

"Yeah, I have to. This commute would suck."

"Any commute in and around D.C. sucks but I agree. You have to move closer. Oh my God, I'm so excited for you. Where are you now?"

"In the truck three hours away." And grateful he had satellite radio and cruise control for the long drive.

"Three hours. I'll be home from work about the time you hit town. Do you want to come over? I've got beef stroganoff in the slow cooker. We could celebrate by looking at some apartment listings online for you. I know the residential areas pretty well. I've had to help some of the new hires find housing."

Dinner with Maggie twice in as many weeks. It was a horrible idea, but when he opened his mouth, he said, "Sure. I'd love to."

He blamed his weakness on the fact he loved her beef stroganoff, to the point he'd even attempted making it on his own.

He'd failed miserably at it but hers was always perfect. There was probably some deep symbolism in that.

He chose not to explore it as he added, "I'll pick up a bottle of Malbec on my way over."

"Perfect. Thanks."

"Sure. No problem." He hated that he knew, and more cared, that her favorite wine was Malbec from the Mendoza region of Argentina. Hated it as much as the fact he, a beer drinker, had started to drink it, and like it too, because of her.

It was a damn good thing he'd have to find an apartment closer to D.C. because this—this whole new strange dynamic between him and Maggie— wasn't doing him any good.

He didn't want to be her friend. He didn't want to be her buddy. He wanted to be her husband. Her lover. The love of her life. The man who put a smile on her face in the morning and had her screaming his name each night.

But all this new stuff—hugging goodbye at the door and sharing meals and good news—wasn't going to cut it.

Nope. All it did was give him hope. Hope he didn't want to feel.

Experience had taught him one thing—the path to Hell was paved with hope.

In spite of that, he hit the accelerator and reset his cruise control for ten miles an hour above the speed limit so he'd get there faster.

Yup. He was definitely on the downhill slope on the road to Hell.

He'd obsessively checked his cell for texts from her since their pizza date. He was racing to get to her now. He'd even started dreaming about her. Dreams that had him waking sweaty and hard and unsatisfied.

There weren't enough miles between Virginia Beach and Washington, D.C. to save him from himself but at least it was a start.

Silas arrived at Maggie's door a few hours later, a bottle of wine in his hand.

There was also a bottle of bourbon he'd picked up and stashed in the truck for later. He had a feeling he was going to need it.

After spending time with her, it felt even more lonely in his apartment.

He reached up to ring the bell. It was just as surreal to ring the doorbell of his former home as it was to enter by the front door instead of pulling the truck into the driveway and going in through the garage.

Of all the many liberties he'd lost in the divorce,

why was he lamenting about his right to enter through the back? Given the new and disturbing sex dreams he'd been having almost nightly about Maggie, he was obviously missing his marital privileges the most.

She pulled the door open and launched into his arms. "Congratulations!"

He sucked in a breath and patted her back with his one empty hand. "Uh, thanks."

Pulling his pelvis a safe distance away from her, he was happy when she broke the embrace and waved him inside.

"Come on in. I snuck out of work early and I've been online. I've found some great options for you that are commuting distance to DHS headquarters."

"Great. Thanks."

It was enough to give a man whiplash having her pressed up against him one minute and then pushing him to move to a city three hours away the next.

Apparently Maggie had no problem with their new status as friends. Which was odd since it wasn't even six months ago that he'd asked her if she'd wanted to grab a bite and she'd said no.

But she had said then that one day they might be able to be friends.

Apparently *one day* had arrived, for her at least, but not for him. She'd been right to begin with. This exes as friends bullshit was too confusing.

He followed her to the kitchen and moved directly to the drawer where the utensils were kept.

The corkscrew was tucked inside, just as it always had been.

So much had changed, while so much remained the same.

Irrationally annoyed by that reality, Silas jammed the sharp metal end into the cork, attacking it with unnecessary vigor while Maggie moved to her computer, still chatting about real estate.

She'd bent at the waist to see the screen, obviously too excited to sit in the chair as she spewed addresses and square footage at him. Meanwhile, all he could concentrate on was how amazing her heart-shaped ass looked and how he wanted to yank those pants down and take her right there, bent over the kitchen table.

*Shit.*

He grabbed a wine glass and filled it, downing half before he took the time to grab a glass for her from the cabinet.

It was going to be a long evening and a long two weeks until he started that job. He couldn't get away from the temptation of the woman he couldn't have soon enough.

# CHAPTER TEN

"Si."

Silas turned to see Chavez leaning into the open doorway of his office. "Sir?"

"I'm on my way to an interagency meeting that I'd like you to sit in on."

"Um, all right. Sure. I'm at your disposal." He closed the lid of his laptop putting to sleep the machine he spent far too many waking moments staring at.

As they walked shoulder-to-shoulder down the hall, Chavez glanced sideways at Silas. "Sorry for the lack of advance warning."

In his ten months at DHS, Silas was getting used to that. Things moved surprisingly fast here.

"It's no problem. Anything you need, I'll make it happen."

Chavez smiled. "That's what I love about you. You're a real team player."

A burst of a laugh escaped Silas. "That's kind of instilled within us in the teams."

"I suppose it would be. Yes." The man grinned. "I'm just not used to it. The leadership in this town seems to be playing for their own team."

Silas knew what Chavez was referring to but chose not to comment on it. He wasn't going to step into that political minefield willingly. To date, he'd managed to avoid it.

It wasn't too hard to do—not take sides or get political.

In the service, he'd fought for the red, white and blue of the stars and stripes.

He was still a SEAL in his heart, even though he was medically retired, and as such he fought on the side of freedom against those who would do that ideal harm around the world and within the borders of the United States and its territories.

In politics however, it did seem to be red versus blue, as if the two couldn't coexist peacefully.

"Do you mind if I ask what this meeting is?" Silas asked as the walk down the hallway stretched on.

Chavez paused at the elevator and pushed the button. "You'll see soon enough."

And with that, Silas's line of questioning was shut down.

Stepping inside the elevator, Chavez pushed the button for the next level up, while Silas wondered why they hadn't just taken the stairs that were right outside his office.

He could feel his muscles atrophy as he sat at that damn desk in the cushy chair with the perfect lumbar support that actually felt good on his back.

His desk job was one reason he went for a run every morning, rain or shine, before showering and heading in to work.

DHS might have turned him into a desk jockey, but it didn't mean he had to feel or look like one.

Chavez led the way down the second hallway of their journey in silence. He finally stopped in front of an office and reached for the knob. Opening the door, he motioned for Silas to walk in ahead of him.

As Silas complied, he found a clue as to why he was in this meeting, because among a dozen others, Maggie was seated at the table.

He swallowed hard and tried to erase his reaction from his expression.

In the months since he'd been hired, the months since he'd worked his way up in the agency to take on more and more responsibilities, he'd avoided Maggie with every ounce of restraint within him.

It was the only way to keep his sanity.

It took about a month after he relocated to D.C. for him to realize he couldn't continue to stalk her movements on Facebook or Instagram to look for hints of what she was doing . . . and with whom. He couldn't keep texting her with any excuse he could find ranging from saying thanks—again—for getting him the interview, to asking about the weather because he saw a storm moving in on her area.

He couldn't because he knew one day there'd be evidence she'd moved on. That she'd started dating again.

Just because he wasn't ready for that yet, and wasn't sure he ever would be, didn't mean she wasn't.

But the reality remained they both worked for DHS. In different offices. In different agencies. But the same organization nonetheless. He just thought her working in Virginia for the OPA and him in D.C. for OPS would keep them apart.

He'd obviously been wrong because there she sat.

Silas glanced at Chavez.

The question must have been clear in his eyes because the man leaned closer and said low, "Is this going to be okay?"

Silas and Chavez had developed a friendship that went beyond that of the typical superior and subordinate relationship.

They'd shared stories and laughs over bourbon at the local bar more times than Silas could count since he'd been hired.

Chavez didn't know details, but he knew Silas and Maggie could work together, be in the same room together, without there being a screaming match between them.

What Chavez didn't realize is that putting them in a room together just ripped the carefully tended scab right off Silas's heart.

"Yeah. It's fine." Silas nodded once to his boss, then turned his attention to Maggie, who watched him with the same beautiful soul-filled eyes he'd stared into so many times while they'd done so many things.

Silas nodded a hello to her as well and glanced at the seating choices. There were two seats left, both of them to the right of Maggie.

To sit next to her would send a message. But not sitting directly next to her would also say something.

The choice wasn't one he wanted to make, so he stepped back so his boss could make the decision.

His time working for the third largest cabinet department in the government had enforced in him the important skill of how to pass the tough things up the chain of command.

Chavez moved forward and pulled out the chair farthest from Maggie. That was it then. Decision made. Silas had no choice but to sit next to her.

Accepting his fate, Silas noticed the uptick in his pulse rate as he slid into the narrow space between Maggie and Chavez to sit in the last empty seat in the room.

Judging by the packed office, everyone who was coming was here. Time to get this damn meeting going.

"Hi." Maggie's whispered word close to his ear sent a chill down his spine.

"Hi," he said, shooting her a quick sideways

glance before focusing on his hands folded on top of the table.

He wished he had something to hold. Coffee. A folder. Anything.

He remembered he had a pen in his pocket, but with no paper that would look stupid to take it out. He would have pulled out his cell phone, but he was used to being in the teams and cell phones weren't allowed in classified meetings.

Was this meeting classified? Hell if he knew. He hadn't even been aware of it until a few minutes ago.

The Deputy Secretary of DHS was seated at the head of the table. She glanced around at the attendees, sitting shoulder-to-shoulder.

"It looks like we're all here so let's get down to business. We're at the final stages of planning the logistics for our multiagency attendance at the World Summit next month in Africa."

At that information, Silas's gaze whipped up to focus on the woman speaking. He sat straighter in his chair, on alert now as he listened for the exact location of this meeting he'd heard nothing about until now.

Why had he heard nothing about it? And why was he here now?

He could only hope the answer to the first question was that this summit hadn't been on his radar because there was no information regarding a threat. But he knew better than that.

Travel to Africa did not come without threats.

Not for non-governmental agencies—which had been proven time and again—nor for governmental ones.

The proof was in how many times Tier One operators had been called in to that region. And now a bunch of agency heads were going to be there for a well-publicized summit and they'd need to be well protected, because the bad guys had plenty of time to coordinate an attack.

"Because of the current political climate around the world and the peace mission of this summit, we've decided to add a representative from the Office of Public Affairs."

*Maggie's office.*

Silas's heart sped as he tried to reason with himself. It didn't mean that she personally would be going. Although why would they have brought her all the way from Virginia Beach for this meeting if she weren't going?

*Shit.*

"Yes, Madam Deputy Secretary. Maggie Branson, our liaison to the Navy, is here. She's slated to represent our office at the summit."

The deputy secretary nodded and turned her attention to Silas's side of the table. "Director Chavez. You'll be representing the Office of Operations Coordination."

"Yes, Madam Deputy Secretary. Along with my second in command, Lieutenant Commander Branson."

Silas cut his gaze to Chavez.

The deputy secretary nodded before turning her attention to the person seated closest to her. "And Science and Technology?"

"Yes, ma'am. Our agency will be represented by the acting under secretary . . ."

Silas ignored what was being discussed at the other end of the table in favor of leaning closer to Chavez. He raised one brow and said just loud enough his boss would be able to hear, "Second in command?"

Chavez smiled. "Something we need to discuss. The position of Deputy Director."

What the hell? Just shy of one year with DHS and he was getting promoted? The enormity and weight of that was as exhilarating as it was unnerving.

"Talk later," Chavez whispered.

"Yes, sir."

Silas tried to pay attention through the rest of the meeting, but after all the bombshells that had hit him since Chavez had pulled him out of his office, what was being discussed paled in comparison.

He was going to this summit, in Africa, as deputy director, along with Maggie. It was a lot to process.

The general logistics—who would be representing each agency—wasn't what he needed to know and apparently that was mainly what this meeting was about.

Silas wanted specifics. How were they

traveling? Through which countries? What security was being provided and by whom during each stage of the trip?

As his thoughts raced, the meeting broke. His mind was still spinning when Maggie's hand on his forearm caught his full attention.

"So, how have you been?" she asked. "We haven't talked in forever."

True. And that had been by his design.

"I'm good. Busy. Working hard." He was babbling and wishing she wouldn't touch him.

It was too tempting to lace his fingers with hers and hold her hand the way he had countless times in the past.

"I know you've been busy." She smiled.

He raised a brow. "How do you know?"

"My boss is friendly with your boss. They talk about you."

Wasn't that interesting. "Do they? And what do they say?"

"That you've really distinguished yourself in the agency and there was a good chance you'd be moving up in the ranks shortly. I see they were right." She smiled.

She'd obviously picked up on Chavez calling him his second in command.

"Silas, walk with me to my office," Chavez said as he pushed his chair back and then stood.

"Yes, sir." Silas glanced at Maggie. As their eyes met, he said, "Um, catch up later?"

She nodded. "Definitely, since we'll be traveling together shortly."

Yes, they would. And shit, he'd taken that trip to Africa, quite a few times, during his years in the SEALs. It wasn't short.

There went his plan to try to avoid her.

"Right. Okay. See you then." He couldn't make his escape soon enough.

Once outside in the hallway, Chavez apparently had something to discuss with him.

"Are you sure you're going to be okay with having your ex-wife on this trip?" Chavez asked.

Silas frowned. "Yeah, I'll be fine."

Chavez nodded, apparently accepting his answer. "Good."

His boss might be satisfied, but Silas wasn't. He still had questions about this whole thing.

"Um, which African nation is hosting this meeting?" Silas asked.

Of all the boring details he'd sat through in that meeting, this was the one that hadn't been mentioned.

"Chad," Chavez said.

Chad? *Shit.* Of all the countries on the continent of Africa, Chad was on his top ten list of places he'd rather not be traveling to with a group of civilians—one of which was Maggie.

Silas sighed. He raised his gaze to Chavez. "What? Somalia wasn't available? Or Borno? Or how about Benghazi?"

Then an attack would be certain instead of just probable and he could prepare accordingly.

Chavez let out a laugh. "I understand your concern, but there's a strong environmental component to this summit, in addition to the peace keeping and humanitarian missions." When he saw what must have been a look of confusion on Silas's face, Chavez continued, "For the past hundred years Lake Chad has been shrinking considerably."

"Ah." Climate change wasn't Silas's department, but keeping people safe was and there weren't many other places they could have chosen that would have made him more worried than this particular region.

At least it wasn't Syria. That thought was small comfort.

Silas knew what he'd be doing between now and the time they left. That was learning everything he could about the logistics of the area and the venue and this damn summit.

"So, about your new position . . ." Chavez began, interrupting Silas's list of things he needed to do to keep the delegation, and his ex-wife, safe in one of the most dangerous regions in the world.

Silas let out a short laugh. "Yes, about that."

Good thing he was used to rolling with the punches because for a governmental organization where he'd assumed things moved notoriously slow, things were sure moving fast for him.

# CHAPTER ELEVEN

The moment the plane touched down, Silas was back in warrior mode—if he'd ever really left it to begin with.

He kept his eyes peeled for anything out of the ordinary. Anything that looked at all suspicious or threatening.

And what the hell was he going to do if he saw something? Hell if he knew because thanks to rules and regulations he was traveling basically unarmed.

He had a few things with him but not what he really wanted—a gun, preferably two.

There was that governmental red tape he'd loved to hate when he was active duty. But now, it was not just annoying, it was dangerous.

Okay, perhaps he wasn't completely unarmed. He had his hands and his brain and almost fifteen years worth of training to draw upon if the shit hit the fan—even so, he'd feel better if he had a weapon.

From what he could see online the Hotel N'Djamena was lovely, with its river front location, multiple outdoor pools and even a whisky bar he might have really enjoyed had it been anywhere else besides Chad.

But Silas was more interested in the other amenities besides the self-proclaimed luxurious spa and outstanding cuisine, such as the hotel's close proximity to the international airport—the less time they spent on the road and vulnerable the better in his opinion.

It was the secure gated entrance he liked best. Though the fact that hotel management felt a gate was not only necessary but also touted prominently on the website told him he was right to be extra cautious. This city and its dangers were no joke.

He hated everything about this trip.

Fuck DHS and their need to attend this thing live and with his wife—*ex*-wife—in tow. Couldn't they all video conference from the office?

That's what modern technology was for—to prevent the need to fly halfway around the world. But instead, when the summit began tomorrow morning they'd all be sitting in a ballroom with five hundred other people waiting for the keynote speaker like a bunch of sitting ducks.

One day at a time. He'd deal with tomorrow. Right now, he had to get everybody safely from the airport to that gated entrance the hotel was so proud of.

The hotel had a dedicated airport shuttle and though he didn't love the idea, they were going to take it.

That shuttle, which was easily identifiable and stuck out amid the other traffic like a sore thumb, made them a well-marked target for attack.

That was on top of the fact Silas didn't know the driver, nor did he know how well, or even *if* he'd been vetted by the hotel.

They could be getting into a vehicle with a suicide bomber for all he knew. But short of frisking the man, there wasn't anything Silas could do.

The one thing Silas *could* do was check the vehicle itself for explosives, which he did even if it did earn him an angry look from the driver.

No doubt Silas's inspection delayed them. Too bad. He didn't give a shit. Let the man scowl all he wanted, they weren't boarding that van until he'd seen inside the engine and beneath the chassis and checked for explosives.

The man spoke enough English that Silas could get across that he wanted to look under the hood. There was a bit of a battle but finally the man complied and popped it open.

After Silas finished with the engine, he moved on to checking beneath the vehicle. Given the expression on the driver's face he was probably lucky the man didn't drive away while he was under there.

When he shimmied out from beneath the van and stood, brushing the dirt off his clothes, he saw Chavez watching him with an expression of amused satisfaction while Maggie was beginning to look worried.

The rest of their little party just looked mainly surprised and confused.

They'd better get used to him doing things like laying on his back beneath a vehicle with a flashlight because on this trip he intended to be more SEAL and less government square ass than they'd come to know him to be at the office.

"We can board," he said.

When the dozen people in their party stared at him unmoving, Chavez took control. "All right, everyone. You heard the man. Get on."

Maggie moved closer. "Is everything all right?"

"Everything's fine," he said. Though silently he added the words *so far*.

"What did you hear? Or did you see something? Why are you worried?" she asked, seeming agitated.

He lifted a brow. "I'm always worried. And no I didn't see or hear anything. Just being cautious."

"Would you tell me the truth if you had?" Maggie asked.

It was a valid question.

Silas considered it for a moment. Would he tell her? The answer was clear. "Yes. I would. I swear."

Keeping her in the dark wouldn't keep her safe. In fact, he liked the group being a little afraid. They'd be more careful. Sometimes fear was a good thing. It could keep you alive.

Maggie watched him for a second and then nodded. "Okay."

She believed him. That was a good sign—not that he was looking for one.

*Crap.* One day of being with her and he was already looking for signs.

This was why he'd avoided her. Now he felt like all that time apart hadn't even happened. He was right back to feeling the combined heartache and hope he'd been riddled with right after the divorce.

He knew he'd never get over the loss of Jonas, but he really had hoped he'd get over Maggie eventually.

How the hell long did it take a man to get over a woman after being with her for so long? He had a feeling he wouldn't like the answer.

Silas boarded the shuttle last and surveyed those inside as he ducked beneath the doorframe. It was tightly packed in there but he'd rather have them all on one vehicle than divided into two.

He searched for a spot he could squeeze in and of course, it was next to Maggie. Fate was definitely conspiring against him.

Bracing himself for the emotional and physical impact sitting next to her would bring, he planted his ass on the edge of the seat, hanging half off so he wouldn't be pressed from shoulder to thigh against the woman he still dreamed about at night.

The driver took off, too fast as far as Silas was concerned, and he had to reach for the seat in front of him.

Finally giving in, he scooted closer to Maggie. He was going to end up on his ass on the floor if he didn't.

He glanced sideways and collided with her blue gaze.

Lips pressed together tight, he averted his eyes and looked out the windows instead. First one side, then the other, searching for threats, as well as getting his bearings.

It wouldn't hurt to be familiar with the route to the airport. He hoped chances were nil things would go so south that he'd have to get them all to the airport on his own and in a hurry—though it could happen. He'd seen too much in the teams to think otherwise.

Maggie softly chuckled next to him. He glanced at her in question.

"Once a team guy, always a team guy." She smiled.

"That obvious?" he asked.

"Only to me," she said, sounding almost sad.

*Only to me*—because she knew him so well. Because they'd shared so much. Three little words but they hurt like hell. They twisted his heart and reminded him what he'd had. What he'd lost.

He drew in a breath and moved his gaze back to

the passing scenery, but as he did he reached out and squeezed her hand. "It's going to be fine."

She squeezed back. "I know."

Such confidence in him. He only hoped he could live up to it—and do what he had to, to get his head out of his ass and off his ex-wife.

They were nearing the hotel. He could see the gates opening up ahead.

As the shuttle navigated slowly between them, he was happy to see it was manned and not automated. Although men were human. They could be bought off, corrupted, killed, replaced . . .

Feeling less good about the manned gatehouse than he had before, he leaned forward and stared at the uniformed employee as the shuttle driver pulled slowly through.

The two men nodded and waved to each other as Silas remained prepared for anything.

His mind turned to another foreign country on this very continent, and another gate that had been left purposely open by someone on the locally hired security force to allow the rebels inside.

He'd spoken with some of the survivors of the Benghazi attack. He'd attended the funerals of those who didn't survive. He knew too many inside facts about the ambush on the US Embassy compound to be complacent now.

Silas should have insisted they set up their own security and not trust the summit organizers to handle it.

They should have their own men manning that

gate. And an overwatch team on the roof and another along the route from the airport to the hotel because even though killing the American delegation would be the cherry on top of the terrorist sundae, any one of the attendees of this damned summit could also be a target.

Silas had a job to do and no tools with which to do it.

*Fuck!* He hated this.

Gripping the back of the seat in front of him, he was set on high alert as he watched and waited.

He jumped at the unexpected touch on his shoulder. Spinning, he found Chavez's face close to his.

"Relax."

Silas shook his head. "You brought me along to protect you."

Chavez laughed. "No, I didn't."

"Then why?" he asked, not believing his boss could be that naïve to think they were safe here.

"You're moving up in the agency and you should be here. And yes, it doesn't hurt that you have experience traveling in the more volatile regions of the world, since so many of our party don't. But you're not here as a bodyguard for me or anyone else, Si. Remember that."

It was that experience that made it impossible for Silas to relax as Chavez ordered.

"Yes, sir," he said to appease his boss, but he had no intention of complying.

Whatever the reason he'd been brought along, he wasn't going to let his guard down or allow anything to happen. Not to anyone, and most certainly not to Maggie.

Or to himself, either.

He hadn't survived what he had in the teams to be taken out now because he treated this trip to Chad like a fucking vacation.

Silas stood the moment the shuttle came to a stop. He didn't wait for the driver to open the sliding side door but instead opened it himself and stepped down to the ground.

Motion caught his eye. He turned and saw Maggie behind him about to climb out.

Silas held up one hand. "Stay." He added, "Please. Just a minute until I make sure it's clear."

She nodded and eased back into her seat. The woman next to her, in the spot against the window and unable to get out until Maggie did, leaned in and whispered something.

Maggie replied and the woman's eyes widened.

Fine. If it took a whispered game of telephone to spread the word that he was a combat experienced operator to make his co-workers heed his advice, so be it.

Keeping his traveling companions a little nervous and a lot more alert would only make his self-appointed job easier.

Squinting against the blinding glare of the Sahara sun, Silas slipped on his sunglasses.

Through the mirrored lenses, he glanced back

toward the gate. It was closed once again. He turned toward the building.

The hotel would serve both as accommodations for them and the meeting place for the summit, meaning that theoretically no one should have to leave the confines of the property until it was time to fly out.

All he had to do was make sure it was well known that it wasn't okay to go wandering around outside the wire—or the gate, as the case may be. No long walks to absorb local culture. No selfies with the sights. No trips to the nearby museums he saw listed on the website.

He really should have addressed everyone. Without the authority to do so, he couldn't lay down rules, but he could give advice. He probably should have done so during the drive while they were captive.

Now it was too late. Pivoting back toward the shuttle he saw everyone had unloaded and were in the process of claiming their luggage from the back as the driver tossed it all to the ground.

Even Maggie had gotten off, though she hung back by the door of the shuttle and watched him.

Good girl. Though no longer *his* girl.

The dull stab that thought caused in his heart set him in motion. He needed to move. To work. To do something besides feel.

He navigated around bags and travelers to Maggie. "Come on. We'll grab your luggage and get checked in. I'll feel better when you're in your room."

Her lips twitched. "Are you going to lock me in my room the whole time we're here to keep me safe?"

"Will you let me?" he asked, only half joking.

She shook her head. "No."

"Didn't think so." He smiled. "I just don't like being out here in the open." Silas glanced once more at the gate.

Her hand on his forearm caught his attention. "I was at those funerals with you. I know what you're thinking."

How was she so intuitive and understanding now, when back when Jonas had died and she'd demanded a divorce she'd been neither?

That thought angered him as much as it reminded him why they were no longer married. She couldn't forgive him then for having to be away doing his job. And he still hadn't forgiven himself.

This was neither the time nor the place for a discussion, even if he had wanted to have one, which he didn't.

Silas tipped his head toward the building. "Go on. I've got the bags."

"I can—" She reached for the handle of her roller suitcase than pulled her hand back when he lifted a brow and kept his hand on it. "Still won't let me carry my own suitcase?"

"Nope," he said with a definitive shake of his head.

Her lips twitched. "Okay. Thank you."

"You're welcome. Now get inside, please." He lifted his chin toward the group already starting to enter the building.

"Yes, sir." She smiled.

The DHS delegation walked in front of him, but that was best. From his vantage point behind the group, he could keep an eye on things.

He glanced at the roof. No motion up there. Not at the moment, anyway. He swept the windows facing the front with his gaze. Nothing caught his eye.

Nothing seemed amiss . . . so why were the hairs on the back of his neck standing up?

# CHAPTER TWELVE

Inside the lobby the hotel looked deceptively normal. It could have been any chain hotel back in the states—except that it wasn't.

Silas didn't let appearances sway him or his actions.

With his sixth sense still screaming in his ear, he wasn't going to let his guard down until they were on the plane and at thirty thousand damn feet up in the air.

Chavez must have already checked in. He walked toward Silas from the direction of the front desk with something that looked like a keycard envelope in his hand.

"Silas."

"Yes, sir."

"I've got a dinner meeting scheduled so you're on your own for tonight. The opening session begins at nine. Can we meet for breakfast tomorrow at, let's say, seven-thirty? Or is that too early?"

Silas smothered his laugh. Anything after sunrise was not what he'd consider early. "Not too early at all. I believe the main restaurant serves breakfast. Should I make reservations?"

Chavez shook his head, smiling. "Thank you, but not necessary. I'll have my assistant handle that."

Silas nodded, still not sure why the hell he was here. It apparently wasn't to attend whatever dinner meeting Chavez was going to tonight. He'd said it wasn't to play bodyguard to him either.

Maybe the opening session would prove enlightening as to why they'd all had to fly to Africa.

*Ridiculous.*

But as long as Maggie had to be here, Silas was glad he was too. Even if she wasn't legally his responsibility any longer, he still felt responsible for her. He had a feeling that would never change.

When Chavez took his leave, after a promise to see him at the restaurant bright and early, Silas turned to Maggie. "Let's get you checked in."

She lifted a brow. "You know, I'll be fine on my own if you have somewhere else to be."

"I know," he said, mostly to make her happy. "But as it turns out I don't have anywhere else to be until seven-thirty in the morning so there's nothing stopping me from helping you get settled in your room."

*Settled. Safely locked inside. Whichever.*

"What's really up with you?" She narrowed her gaze at him and continued, "And don't say nothing. I know you too well for you to lie to me."

Drawing in a breath through his nose while he pressed his lips together, Silas considered his answer.

He opted for the truth, a surprise decision even to himself. "I've just got a bad feeling."

She pinned him with a stare for a moment, before saying, "All right."

He lifted his brow. "All right? That's it?"

Maggie raised one shoulder. "You might have thought I was in the dark while we were married and you were still in the teams, but I wasn't. Team guys talk to their wives, whether they're supposed to or not. And their wives talk to each other. I heard about how one of your *feelings* saved the team from an ambush. I'm not about to doubt you now."

That was quite a revelation. He drew in a breath and let it out in a huff. God willing this time the nagging in his brain was wrong. Either way, he didn't want to worry Maggie.

"It's probably nothing," he said.

"Yeah, right. Probably." She shot him a look he couldn't quite read but he was pretty sure the subtext of her tone said he should stop trying to bull shit her.

She was right. She did know him too well for him to lie to her. He laughed at being busted doing just that.

"Come on. I can't wait to see what the rooms look like. Maybe you have a view of the river."

"And a balcony," she added hopefully.

He smothered a snort. There'd be no balcony if he had anything to say about it. He fully intended to tell the clerk no balconies for either of them because if he were going to break into a room that would be just the way he'd do it. Climb right down from the roof and onto the balcony.

"Uh, yeah. Hopefully," he lied and then turned his back to Maggie and faced the front desk attendant. "We're both checking in. Separate rooms but on the same floor, if possible."

Being on the same floor would help ease his mind slightly.

He shot Maggie a glance and then leaned in closer to the clerk and kept his voice low as he added, "And can they be rooms *without* balconies, please?"

Shortly after, keycards in hand and her suitcase in tow, Silas led Maggie to the elevator and pushed the button.

"Do you want to go to your room and drop off your stuff?" she asked when they got off the elevator and he turned in the direction of her room.

"I will. Later. Let's get you settled in first."

If he really had moved on, like he'd hoped he would have by now, he would have insisted on sleeping in her room. On the floor if there was only one bed, just to make sure she was safe.

As things stood, he couldn't do that. He couldn't stop thinking of her as his wife, his to protect, his to love. But even though he couldn't seem to get it through his thick head that she was none of those things any longer thanks to the divorce, he shouldn't spend the night in her room.

He'd have to settle for knowing she was double locked safely inside whenever he said goodnight to her later.

She opened the door and he pushed past her, checking out the room, evaluating it for safety.

By the time he turned back to the doorway, he saw she'd steered the suitcase into the closet.

She'd also taken off the jacket she'd traveled in and hung that from the rod, leaving her curves in full view.

He yanked his gaze off the tempting lines of her body and back up to her face.

"Am I allowed to go down to the restaurant to eat dinner?" she asked, one brow cocked high.

His lips twitched from the attitude she didn't even try to temper, but instead leveled right at him.

"You're allowed," he said. Even though he actually would prefer if she stayed safely locked in her room.

"Would you like to join me?" she asked. "Or do you have to eat with Director Chavez?" she added.

Her invitation took him aback. Yes, she'd invited him over to eat pizza, but that was out of pity that one night. And then again the night he'd gotten hired, but that was to celebrate and find him an apartment online.

What was her reason for this invitation?

"Uh, no. He's meeting with someone else." And there went his excuse to avoid eating with her, if he'd wanted one. But he didn't. He'd prefer to know she was safe with his own eyes. "Yeah. Sure. We can grab something to eat if you're hungry."

*To know she was safe.* Even he didn't believe his own excuse.

He wanted to be with her, plain and simple. Which was exactly why he shouldn't do it.

"Um, actually I'm kind of starving. Can we go now?" she asked.

He laughed. His woman—make that his *ex-*woman—always could eat.

She would pack away the food without hesitation or shame right from the first time he'd met her. No eating like a bird while on a date for her. It was one of the first things he'd loved about her. One of the things he still loved about her.

"Yeah, I could eat too. Let's go down." He'd dropped his backpack on the floor just inside the door when he first came in. "Mind if I leave my stuff here and grab it after we eat?"

There was no doubt he was walking her back to her room and making sure it—and she—were secured.

"Sure." She grabbed a small purse out of her carry-on bag. "Anything if it means I get fed faster."

She grinned, making him laugh again.

Okay, they were doing this.

After all the months where he purposefully avoided contact with her through any means, he was willingly going to sit opposite this woman in a restaurant for the next hour.

Just the two of them. Like a frigging date. With his ex-wife. Fucking fabulous.

Drawing in a breath, he steeled his resolve.

He could do this. Survive one dinner with Maggie and not completely fall back in love with her.

*Fuck.* Who was he kidding? He'd never fallen out of love with her.

# CHAPTER THIRTEEN

Silas made it through dinner somehow.

Actually, it wasn't as hard as he'd anticipated. Fodder for small talk was all over the place.

They watched the diverse mix of people coming and going through the restaurant even at the odd hour.

They talked about the food they ordered and then had the excuse to not talk at all as they ate.

He had plenty to occupy him and lots to talk about other than the one subject he didn't want to touch—their failed marriage.

And, of course, there was his other not so little task of evaluating everyone and everything as a possible threat. Given how much of his mental capacity that occupied, Silas had to wonder how much of their discussion he'd missed.

Maggie didn't say anything if he had lagged a bit in replying or keeping up his end of the conversation. But he sure as hell must have missed something because as he walked her to her door, there was an unmistakable vibe radiating off her.

She glanced at him sideways and if he wasn't completely off base, she'd just looked him up and down through narrowed eyes.

What the hell?

Was he going crazy? Or was she giving him *that* look. The look that, when they'd been married, meant *let's go to bed early tonight*.

There was one problem—they were no longer married.

Actually, there was a second problem. What if he were imagining things and she didn't want him at all? Maybe she was just tired. Jetlag was a bitch and they had traveled all day.

Was she tipsy? How many glasses of wine had she had?

He'd had zero alcohol to drink. He hadn't wanted to have his senses or his response time impaired in any way in case shit went down.

As Maggie got out her key card and moved toward the door, he reviewed the night. She'd commented on how the red wine she'd ordered was very good. But he thought she'd only had that one glass. In fact, he was fairly certain of it.

So what was this vibe between them?

Silas mentally gave himself a shake. Wishful thinking on his part, that's what it was. A result of being celibate for way too long.

And while he was obsessing over the imaginary chemistry with his ex-wife, he was ignoring the possible dangers that surrounded them.

Reaching out, he took the key card from her just as she was about to slide it into the door slot.

"May I?" he asked.

"Of course." She smiled, but it was somehow more than a smile.

*Crap.* He needed to get inside, make sure the room was clear and then figure out what was going on between them, in that order.

Safety first. Delusional sex fantasies later.

He slipped in the card and watched the light turn from red to green. Turning the knob, he glanced back at her. "Wait right inside the doorway while I check the room."

Her brows rose. "All right."

He moved inside, flipping on the lights first before checking behind the door and motioning Maggie in.

She hesitated. "Door open or closed?" she asked, holding on to it as she hovered in the opening.

"Closed." He didn't need someone grabbing her from the hallway while he checked the closet and the shower stall.

"All righty." There was amusement in her voice. He chose to ignore it.

Once he'd made sure the room was safe, he turned back to face her. "Okay."

She had her arms folded as she leaned against the door, watching him. "You sure? There's no one hiding behind the curtains? Want to check that first before I come all the way in?"

His lips twitched as she clearly mocked his security measures. "No one's behind the curtains. I'd see their feet."

"Oh, yes. Of course." She pushed off the door and moved toward him, planting both palms flat on his chest.

Rising on tiptoe, she pressed a kiss to his cheek and then stayed close, her lips to near to his. "Thank you for watching out for me."

If something had changed between them, no one had bothered to tell him.

All he knew was that they were still legally divorced and he was still living in a rental alone. Sleeping every night alone. Eating dinner in front of the television alone. And that was all because of her wanting the divorce.

So what in the ever loving hell was this about?

He glanced down to where she touched him. Then at the face of the woman he'd like to strip bare and run his hands all over, even if it was the worst idea he'd ever had.

Silas pressed his hands over hers where they rested on his shirt. "Mags. What's going on?"

She lifted her shoulders.

He drew in a breath, fighting against the

tightness in his chest at how achingly good it felt to have her this close. How much better it would feel to slide into this woman.

"It wasn't all that long ago I was at the house and had mentioned if you wanted to grab a bite to eat. You'd said no," he said.

"That was right after the divorce. It's been a year. And we've had meals together since then."

"I know." Meals. Not sex, but if he wasn't crazy that was exactly what she was hungry for now. "Tonight feels like more than eating a meal together."

"Yeah." Those eyes, liquid pools of blue he could drown in, captured his gaze.

He swallowed hard.

"What's changed?" he asked, genuinely interested in hearing the answer because he'd love nothing more than to tumble Maggie into that big bed behind them and pretend the last few years hadn't happened.

"I've been seeing someone—"

*Seeing someone? What the fuck?*

"What?" He took a step back, feeling torn between wanting to punch something or vomit.

"No. Not like that." Maggie closed the space between them, grabbing his hands again. "It's a therapist."

"Oh." He let out a breath and willed his racing pulse to slow.

"She suggested this group. They meet once a week. It's for parents who've lost children."

The thought of talking every week about Jonas was enough to have the acid rising in the back of this throat.

He pressed his lips together and nodded. "I'm glad it's working for you."

Now was the time she'd suggest he go to this group too. Or to one like it in D.C..

And when he said no, that he'd rather not spill his guts in a room of strangers on a weekly basis, the same old fight would be resurrected between them.

It had been a nice fantasy—making love to this woman again, for real and not just in his dreams. Them getting back together. Making a fresh start. But it was just that. A fantasy.

They hadn't been able to work things out then. They wouldn't be able to now.

Her gaze held his as he braced for the inevitable argument between them.

She drew in a breath and said, "I go to this group and I sit there and I listen to them tell their stories. Every week. And the one thing so many of them have in common is the blame. They all blame someone or something for the loss of their child. Sometimes it's themselves. Sometimes it's someone else. But as I sit there and listen I keep thinking, consistently, it's no one's fault. It's horrible but you can't place blame. It just . . . happened."

Maggie drew in a breath, clearly shaken by the

discussion. After biting her lip, she met his gaze again.

"It took a while. Months," she said. "But I was up there telling my story—our story—and I heard it, the blame. And for the first time since it happened I thought, it was nobody's fault. It's just . . . happened."

There were tears in her eyes. Hell, there was a mist in his own eyes as he felt her hands tremble. Or was it his hands that shook as he held hers?

His throat tight, he stayed silent as she continued, "I'm sorry, Silas. I blamed you and I was wrong. I'm so, so sorry. Can you forgive me?"

Not trusting his voice, he nodded as he drew her close, clutching her to him.

It felt so good. Not just having her in his arms, but having her forgiveness. More than that, having her permission to forgive himself.

"Maybe I need to check out this group," he said as he buried his face against her hair.

She pulled back, eyes wide. "Would you really? Would you come with me?"

He was as shocked as his desire to go as she appeared to be by his saying it. "Yes. Once. We'll see how that goes. Good enough?" he asked through the emotions making his heart race.

"Good enough." Maggie's eyes narrowed. She drew in a shaky breath through her mouth as her gaze dropped to his lips. She brought her focus back up to his eyes. "Si."

"Yeah?"

"Don't go to your room."

He knew what she was asking.

It wasn't fear that made her not want to be alone tonight. In fact, it seemed he might be the only one worried about what could happen while they were in Chad.

This woman in his arms wanted him to stay the night for a completely different reason and if he wasn't completely delusional, that motivation was lust, pure and simple.

And what was he going to do about it?

He wanted her more than anything. Needed her more than air to breathe. But he wanted all of her. Her love. Her heart. Her soul. Not just her body for the night.

She might not want that too.

What was it going to do to him to have her tonight and then possibly have to watch her walk back out of his life when they returned to Virginia?

"Stay. Please," she said.

Silas sucked in a breath. Fuck the pain losing her after having her would surely bring.

He threw common sense to the wind and slammed his mouth against hers.

# CHAPTER FOURTEEN

They hadn't done this in so long. Since long before the divorce had been finalized and it had been a year since he'd signed those papers.

Even so, Maggie felt the same beneath his hands. Tasted the same against his tongue. Looked the same as her eyes drifted closed when he kissed her.

But there were subtle changes too. Little differences. Things that messed with his head even as he peeled off her clothes to expose the body he craved.

Beneath the clothes she wore, he found purple underwear and a matching bra.

Purple lingerie. On the woman who'd always only owned basic beige and black undergarments for all the years they'd been married.

His mind went to bad places, wondering whom she'd bought this for. Or worse, who might have bought it for her.

As he stared at the color he couldn't ignore, his hand frozen on the dip of her waist halfway between the two items, she grabbed his head and pulled his mouth down to hers.

Her tongue against his was enough to push those thoughts aside as his cock strained behind the confines of his pants.

She tugged at his clothes.

Impatient to get him naked, was she? Good. He liked that thought.

If he was going to jump head first into a bad idea, at least he wasn't alone in it.

She let out a frustrated groan when he rolled off her.

His lips twitched with a smile as he sat on the edge of the bed and glanced back at her. "Hang on, baby."

He reached down to untie the laces on his footwear of choice—the brand of multi-sport shoes he'd worn for years in the teams whenever the terrain didn't demand boots.

Making the mistake of glancing back at her again as he tugged off one sock, he saw the need in her eyes. He needed her just as badly.

He stripped off the second sock and tossed it to the floor, then reached for his belt, struggling to get it open as his hands fumbled.

He'd traveled in comfort—for him that was

tactical pants.

He was about to get what he'd dreamed about for the past year. What he'd had for so many years with this woman and sorely missed, yet his mind spun with random shit like his pants? He was obviously nervous.

Nervous. About being with the woman he'd shared a bed with for over a decade. It was nuts. But this whole thing was crazy. The divorce. This— whatever this was. Reconciliation? One-night stand?

He didn't know what to call it and decided to give up trying to label what this was between them.

Silas stood and tossed his shirt to the floor . . . and saw her eyes sweep his bare torso.

When he pushed his pants down his legs, followed by his underwear, her gaze moved lower, to the bobbing hard length that sprang free.

Reason took a backseat as need took over.

He crawled onto the bed. She spread her legs and made room for him between them. In this position, his length nudged at her entrance.

His body covering hers, their faces were so close he could hear the hitch in her breath as he pushed inside.

Sliding into her felt like coming home . . . and it went way too fast.

He'd barely begun when it ended too soon.

She felt too good and he'd denied himself for too long. He felt his climax coming, barreling down on him like a freight train, and he had no hope of stopping it.

His spine bowed as he slammed his eyes closed and felt the pulsing begin. He held deep and rode out the waves.

Coming inside her rocked him to the core. Shook him body and his soul.

Even after the last throb had ended, it took him time to recover—at least physically. There was going to be no recovering from this emotionally.

Then there was nothing for him to do except apologize.

Still breathing heavy while trying not to crush her beneath him, he said, "I'm sorry. It's been a long time."

Her lips bowed in a smile. "I'm glad."

He laughed. "Glad I took thirty seconds to come?" he joked and hoped that was actually an exaggeration and not the truth.

Her expression turned serious. "It's been a really long time for me too."

*A really long time.* He gauged what that could mean. Since the last time they'd been together?

God, he hoped so. He wasn't crazy enough to ask. He was too damn happy to ruin this moment with thoughts of another man touching her.

But a thought flew into his brain that managed to suck away a good portion of his joy anyway. "Shit. Are you still on birth control?"

He hadn't even thought to ask. He hadn't had to since after Jonas had been born.

"Yes. Don't worry."

"Oh. Okay. Good."

*Shit.* Why was she still on birth control? Maybe *a really long time* didn't mean as long as he'd hoped.

She raised her hand to touch his face. "The doctor suggested I stay on it to help with my irregular cycle."

Maggie knew him too well. He couldn't hide anything from her. At least not his thoughts about this. He didn't care she could read him so easily. He was too relieved by her answer about why she'd stayed on the pills.

He rolled off her, stood and turned back to reach for her hand.

"Where are we going?" she asked.

"To the shower."

They had a day's worth of travel to wash away, as well as the remnants of some mediocre sex. But after that, he owed her an orgasm—or two.

There were parts of her he thoroughly enjoyed and he had every intention of getting intimately reacquainted with them tonight.

He intended to remind her how good they'd been together, even if it took him until morning to do it.

# CHAPTER FIFTEEN

Chavez lifted one hand high at the table where he was already seated.

Silas made his way across the restaurant and pulled out the chair. "Good morning. Sorry I'm late."

His boss shook his head. "You're not. I was early."

True, but Silas was usually the first to arrive. He prided himself on it. He'd just been a little busy last night *not* sleeping.

He'd slipped out of bed early and, so he wouldn't wake her, he'd grabbed his backpack and snuck out of Maggie's room.

Back in his own room he'd showered quick and dressed for the summit.

"You have a good night?" Chavez asked.

Guilty, Silas whipped his gaze up from where he'd been glancing at the breakfast menu. "Uh. Yeah. I had a good meal at the restaurant last night."

"Yes. I saw you and Maggie there. You two certainly looked . . . amicable." Chavez smirked.

Silas couldn't even give his standard reply, that they were friends. After last night he didn't know what the fuck they were. Friends with benefits maybe?

Hell, he'd enjoyed the benefits too much to question it here and now. But later, when they were home, they were going to have to talk. And hopefully, they'd be doing more of what they'd done last night. Three times.

He glanced up and saw Chavez's smirk.

*Shit.* His thoughts were probably written all over his damn face. One year out of the SEALs and he'd lost his edge. Silas couldn't hide shit anymore, from anyone apparently.

Time to move on from this topic and on to a new conversation. "So I went over the agenda for today and tomorrow."

"I'm sure you did." Chavez smiled. "You don't do anything unprepared."

Not true. He'd taken the interview at DHS unprepared. He'd toppled into bed with Maggie unprepared. The first had worked out pretty well so far. He only hoped the second did too.

The rest of the breakfast, thank God, was spent

talking about the summit.

Silas tried to get as much out of his boss as he could regarding the security precautions that had been taken given the number of foreign delegations gathered there.

It was an exercise in frustration. Either Chavez didn't know much or—worse—not much had actually been done to ramp up security.

Sure, he could spot a bodyguard a mile away and a few of the highest level attendees had them, but close personal security wasn't what he was looking for. He wanted to see this hotel's grounds locked down and guarded like Fort Knox while they were there. It was apparent that wasn't going to happen.

In spite of the nagging feeling in his gut, Silas still managed to get down a plate of toast and eggs and too much coffee during the breakfast.

He was more than happy the menu seemed catered toward foreigners, and Americans in particular, and served basic food in decent portions.

At least he'd eat well on this trip, though he certainly didn't mind not having slept well last night, given the reason.

He wondered if Maggie was awake yet. He glanced at his watch and realized how late it had gotten. The opening session started in fifteen minutes. She'd be up, dressed and probably finding a seat in the ballroom.

They should do the same. But shit . . . he felt a twisting in his lower gut that had nothing to do with worry and everything to do with the coffee he'd consumed.

"Um, we should probably get moving," he said to Chavez.

"Ready when you are." The man had already signed the meal to his room so there was no reason to delay.

And as the pressure in his bowels increased, Silas was more than ready to get going. He glanced at his watch again. He had time to get upstairs to his room, handle his business in the privacy of his own bathroom, and then get back down to the summit.

"I gotta run up to my room for like two minutes. I don't want to hold you up. Do you wanna go on in and I'll find you?" he asked.

Chavez nodded. "Sure. I'll save you a seat."

"Perfect. Thanks."

Plan in place, Silas rode the elevator up to his floor without any problem. It seemed the attendees were all coming down for the opening session and he was the only one heading up so there wasn't a wait at the elevator.

Up in his room, and feeling much better after the pit stop, he was about to head back down when his cell buzzed.

He pulled it out with one hand, while reaching for the doorknob with the other. When he saw Maggie's name on the text alert he smiled and dropped his hand from the knob.

After he unlocked the phone and saw her words, that smile faded quickly.

## SHOOTER IN THE BALLROOM

What the fuck?

He looked around the room, instinct having him searching for a gun that wasn't there.

Had he misinterpreted her message? No. He couldn't have. There was no other explanation for what she'd written.

They were under attack and he was unarmed. But not completely. He lunged for the closet where he'd tossed his backpack.

Inside he had everything he was legally allowed to travel with and might conceivably need. Flashlight. Lock pick. Tactical rope. A short fixed blade knife that would be in compliance with TSA rules. A multi-tool. First aid kit. NVGs—not the real good night vision goggles he'd used in the teams, but good enough.

If he'd been in tactical pants he would have stuffed everything into the pockets. But he was in a fucking suit and didn't want to take the time to change, so he grabbed the backpack, zipped it shut and threw the strap over his shoulder.

He'd already taken his clothes and toiletries out so the pack was empty of everything except his stripped down kit. It wasn't what he was used to going into a mission with, but it would have to do.

Hell, he'd find a security guard and relieve the man of his weapon if he had to. He had no doubt it would be of more use in his own trained, combat-experienced hands than in the control of whoever the hotel hired.

His key card was already in his pocket, in case he needed to get back inside quick. He was armed with everything he had in his possession at the moment, but the one thing he needed and didn't have was information.

He didn't want to risk Maggie's life by asking her for details. She'd managed to slip out a single text without the shooter noticing but he wasn't sure that would remain the case.

That Chavez hadn't also texted told him the situation might be bad down there. With no time to waste, he typed in three words, then added three more before he hit send.

*On my way. I love you.*

As he shoved the cell into his pocket, he didn't let himself think those might be the last words she ever got from him.

Slowly he opened the door and peered into the hall. He pulled the door open wider and leaned out, looking first left and then right.

Seeing it was clear, he ran for the emergency stairs. He couldn't risk standing there like a fool with nothing but a knife and a backpack if the elevator doors opened onto one of the shooters.

How many attackers were there? Maggie's text had been singular, not plural, but he wasn't going to rely on that.

Very aware he hadn't felt another text alert come through from her, he ran faster, leaping over the last three steps at each landing rather than taking them one at a time.

Finally he was at the door that would open onto the ballroom level.

He doubted the attackers, if there were more than one, had someone watching the emergency stairs. The stairwell was too far from the elevators and the ballroom entrance. He knew because he'd swung by to check out the layout on his way down to breakfast this morning.

Silas grabbed the doorknob and eased open the stairwell door, pressing his eye to the crack. He saw a kid dressed in a white apron running toward him.

As far as he could see the kid was young and unarmed. Probably kitchen help. Maybe a busboy.

Silas flattened himself against the wall and waited. When the door opened he reached out and hauled the kid back against him with one hand covering his mouth and the other twisting his arm behind him.

The kid struggled for a second then went still.

"Do you speak English?" he asked.

The kid nodded.

"I'm going to ease my hand away from your mouth. If you scream I'm going to break your neck. Understand?"

After a pause, the kid dipped his head once.

"Good." Silas moved his hand and hooked his elbow around the kid's neck, applying just enough pressure to scare him, but not so much he couldn't talk or breathe. "Tell me what's happening in the ballroom."

"There are men with guns."

"How did you see them?" he asked.

"I was supposed to go inside and check the water and glasses. I opened the door. I saw one man with a gun. I heard the other shouting at the people."

"They didn't see you?" Silas asked.

"No. I'd opened the side door quiet so I wouldn't bother the people."

That made sense, but Silas still wasn't ready to exonerate this kid of any guilt.

He needed more information. "How many men?"

"Two, I think. I don't know."

"What kind of gun did he have?"

"A big gun. I didn't see the other man."

"You said you heard him. What was he saying?"

"He told them to get on the floor and put their hands on their head."

Which was why Maggie couldn't reply to his text.

One more question, for his own comfort more than anything else. "Was anyone hurt?"

The kid shook his head. "I don't know. I didn't see. I don't think so. I heard no gunshots."

Silas blew out a breath. That was the one piece of good news.

He probably had as much information about the attackers as he was going to get out of this kid, but the boy would still be able to help him more.

As an employee, he would know this hotel. All of it. The service areas, not just the public areas. It was a long shot the kid would know about the hotel security but Silas could ask that too.

He heard sirens. Someone had called the police.

The sound of automatic gunfire had him stiffening. The sound didn't come from the direction of the ballroom, but rather from down the stairs. The lobby.

The police must be here but the bad guys had obviously put a gunman at the entrance to prevent them coming in.

"Are there security guards inside the hotel?" he asked the boy.

He shook his head. "There is one outside."

"Yeah. At the gate. I know." Silas sighed.

*Think!* What could he do with what he had?

His eyes widened when he thought of something that might help him.

The NVGs. It might be daytime but that ballroom had no windows. If the lights went out it would be black as night. The bad guys wouldn't have night vision goggles for a daytime attack, but Silas did.

There'd be light switches all over the damn room. He couldn't get inside to kill the lights, but maybe he could do something better. Kill the power.

He loosened his hold on the kid, turning the boy to face him. "Do you know where the electrical panel is?"

The boy's brows drew together in a frown.

From the recesses of his mind, Silas pulled out his limited knowledge of Arabic. Luckily the word for electricity was one he'd had to learn, given some of the places he'd been.

In a mangled mix of English and Arabic, he repeated the request to the boy. Finally his eyes widened and he nodded.

"You know where it is?" Silas asked, afraid to get excited, all while knowing every second that ticked by could mean lives. And one of those lives at stake was Maggie's.

He'd lost Jonas. He wasn't going to lose her too.

"Yes, I know," the boy said.

"Can you show me?" Silas asked.

"Yes." He nodded with more vigor than before.

Silas hated having to put his faith in this kid. But he was out of options. He had to trust the kid whether he liked it or not.

Resigned, he said, "Show me."

The kid pointed toward the door he'd come through. "That way."

On the second floor where there were at least two gunman? Silas blew out a breath.

Could he trust this kid? He didn't know if the boy was involved somehow with whoever had taken control of the building. The kid was young but he was fighting age. He could lead Silas right into an ambush.

"Where exactly? Tell me."

"A room. Small. We keep . . ." The kid pressed his lips together visibly searching for the word that escaped him. Finally he rubbed his fingers on his apron and said, "Cloth?"

"Linens?"

The kid nodded.

"You've seen the electrical box there?"

The boy nodded again.

A linen closet near the ballroom. That made sense. It could very well have the electrical panel in it that controlled the lights inside. He'd soon find out.

"Okay. Let's go. You're going to take me there. Not one word. Understand?"

Wide-eyed the kid nodded again.

Not completely trusting him, Silas kept a tight hold on the kid's slim arm as he eased open the door with his free hand.

The boy hung back. He couldn't blame him. The kid had been running away from the gunman when Silas had grabbed him. And now he was asking the kid to go back toward the danger.

The hallway was empty. Luck was on their side.

Silas motioned the kid forward. "Which way?"

The kid pointed to the right, away from the main doors. Perfect.

They moved fast and quiet. The kid, young and underweight, was quick and light on his feet.

Finally they reached a door. The boy glanced at Silas and pointed to the door.

Silas reached out but the knob wouldn't turn. He looked at the boy.

"They lock it," he said quietly. "People steal."

The manager must carry the key and only open it when necessary. That was fine. Silas was carrying his own set of keys.

Swinging his backpack off his shoulder, he dropped to one knee on the floor, pulling the kid down with him.

He had his pack unzipped and his lock pick set out in seconds. It didn't take much longer than that to open the lock, all as the kid watched, wide-eyed.

With the door open, Silas pulled the boy to his feet as he stood. He flipped on the lights and moved inside the room, taking the boy with him and closing the door behind them.

One glance told him the boy had been correct. Half hidden behind a shelving unit was the electrical panel. He opened the cover and saw the circuit breakers inside.

He set his bag on the shelf and reached inside, pulling out the NVGs. He was going to have to be fast. Kill the power and get into the ballroom through the side door while the gunmen were still disoriented . . . and before they opened fire on the hostages.

Silas slid the rope into his pocket, and slipped the NVGs over his head, leaving the lenses flipped up.

He looked at the boy. "I'm going to turn off the lights then go into the ballroom and take care of the gunmen. You stay here and hide. Okay?"

Nodding, the kid looked terrified as his gaze tracked the knife Silas took out of his backpack. Good. Maybe he was scared enough to do as he was told.

"Okay. Going dark." After pulling the backpack's straps over his arms, Silas held the sheathed knife between his teeth and used both hands to flip all the circuit breakers off.

With the night vision goggles flipped down and the knife in his hand, he pulled open the door and headed into the hall, running for the side entrance to the ballroom.

# CHAPTER SIXTEEN

Inside the ballroom was chaos.

Silas heard it even before he could see it through the green glow of the NVGs.

It was easy enough to locate the first gunman. He was standing and yelling while waving what looked like an AK-47.

He was near the sidewall, but facing the room, not the door. Perfect.

In a few long strides Silas covered the distance between them. A few seconds later, he silently eased the gunman to the floor.

He relieved the man of his weapon and his ammo as the life's blood drained from his limp body.

Silas couldn't ignore the hostages that surrounded him. Even in the dark, they'd have heard the gurgling of the dying man.

"I'm here to help," he said barely above a whisper. "Stay down. Stay quiet."

Rising on his knees so he could see over the chairs blocking his view, he turned his attention to locating the second gunman.

The kid had said he'd heard him the room but hadn't seen him. Silas saw why. He was all the way on the other side of the room by the main entrance to the ballroom where there were three sets of double doors.

It was too far for him to make his way across the room to take him out with the knife like he had his partner, but Silas had a better weapon now.

Silas raised the gun. He didn't have much time.

The gunman had noticed his partner's sudden silence and wasn't taking it well. He was visibly agitated, yelling while swinging the weapon wildly.

Silas hated taking a shot in a room full of civilians. Desperate people were unpredictable. Someone could decide to attempt an escape in the dark and jump up into his line of fire.

He had no choice. Finger on the trigger, he blew out a breath and squeezed.

The asshole attackers had no suppressors on their weapons like Silas was used to. The sound was deafening against his ear. The hostages didn't react any better to the noise. He heard screams, a few sobs, but none of it mattered because the man in his sights crumbled to the ground.

Silas knew better than to expose himself or the

hostages without confirming the target was disabled.

Keeping low, he skirted the hostages on the ground and made his way as fast as he could to the location of the second gunman. When he got to him, he found the man down but still alive.

He took control of the weapon then flipped the man onto his stomach and planted his knee in his back.

It would have been very satisfying to end this bastard's life with a double tap to the head, but Silas had to be satisfied with tying him up. He could be a source of valuable information regarding the attack. Who'd planned it. Why.

Rocking back on his knees, Silas took a breath.

This thing was far from over. He couldn't be sure there weren't more attackers in the room, lying in wait.

There was still the gunman in the lobby keeping the authorities outside. On top of that, he was in possession of two weapons and if the authorities did make it inside he'd be the first one in their crosshairs when the lights came on because they wouldn't know he was on their side.

Silas was used to having backup. He could operate alone but he was better as part of a team.

He could use a team to back him up right about now.

Maybe he had one. There were those few bodyguards he'd spotted with some of the summit attendees. They could hold the room and keep everyone inside safe while he went to deal with the gunman in the lobby.

The room was loud with conversation, crying, cell phones beeping and buzzing, all as the hostages began to figure out they were no longer in immediate danger.

From his position on the floor, Silas shouted. "Quiet!"

The group, amazingly, listened and quieted down.

"I'm Lieutenant Commander Silas Branson. Formerly of the US Navy. Currently with the US Department of Homeland Security. The two gunmen are down but I need help. Who here is carrying a gun?"

"I am." A voice with a foreign accent came to him from across the room.

"Me too." That answer was from closer.

Two. That was good enough.

"All right. I need you two to maintain control of this room and protect these people until I can deal with the shooter in the lobby and determine if there are any more."

"We can not see," one man said.

"Yeah. That was me. I killed the electric. I'll turn it back on."

The lobby had windows so the electricity being off wouldn't help him downstairs anyway. He'd have to use the element of surprise and the AKs he'd acquired.

He needed to go, but there was one thing he needed to know first. "Is Maggie Branson in the room?" he shouted.

"I'm here." Her voice broke as she spoke.

"You okay?" He stood to search for her but in a room where it seemed everyone was suddenly moving, he couldn't find her.

"She's unharmed, Si. Shaken up, but I've got her," Chavez called from the middle of the room. "I'll take care of Maggie until you're back. You just go and get that last bastard and get us the fuck out of here."

"Yes, sir." He wanted nothing more.

Silas eased open one of the main doors. The hallway was still clear. He skirted around the corner and pushed open the linen room door.

The boy let out a yelp.

"Just me, kid." Silas took a small flashlight out of his pocket and flipped up the NVGs.

By the beam of the penlight he navigated to the electrical panel and started flipping the breakers back on.

When the lights came up he spared a quick glance backward. "Stay here."

"You didn't get them?" the boy asked.

"I did. Two, but there's more."

The kid's ever-expressive eyes widened. "You'll get them all."

Silas nodded. The kid was right. He would, or

die trying.

Out in the hall, it was all he could do to stop himself from peeking into the ballroom just to see with his own eyes that Maggie was safe.

He'd have to trust Chavez.

Silas moved fast down the hall, stopping at the door to the stairs. He stilled and listened for any indication that the attacker might be on his way upstairs to check on his partners.

Hearing none, he eased open the door and leaned over the staircase.

With the coast clear, he treaded as silently down as he could in the damn leather dress shoes he was wearing.

If they all got out of this thing unscathed, he was going to discuss the impracticality of regular business wear during an attack with his boss.

Silas pressed against the wall by the door to the first floor and listened.

He heard a man speaking, fast and loud. In between his foreign words was the sound of a woman sobbing.

She spoke in a regional dialect that made it hard for Silas to understand her words, but he felt the tone behind them.

Fear. Panic. If he wasn't mistaken, she was begging for her life.

Now would have been another good time for his non-existent team to back him up.

Hell, he wasn't greedy. Never mind a full SEAL team. He'd settle for a smoke bomb or a flash bang right about now. He needed a diversion.

He remembered his backpack.

He'd picked up a pack of matches from the bowl filled with them on the hostess desk in the restaurant last night. He'd tossed them into his pack in his room when he'd emptied his pants pockets before showering this morning.

Glancing up, he saw the sprinkler head.

With any luck . . . he struck a match and reached up, holding the flame right below the small metal valve.

Amid flashing lights and a deafening alarm, water began to spray from the device.

Diversion accomplished. He loved when things worked out according to plan.

With a renewed surge of adrenaline pulsing through his body, he squinted against the water hitting him and eased open the door a crack. The noise from the lobby grew louder—clearer now that the door was open.

Though the alarm sounded throughout the building, the sprinklers going off seemed to be confined to the stairwell.

He slipped through the door and down the hall until he could see a portion of the lobby and the concierge desk conveniently located nearby.

The gunman was losing his shit by the time Silas got eyes on him from his vantage point.

Whoever the attackers were, they didn't respond well to adversity. They'd make shitty SEALs, that was for sure, but the gunman's agitation worked in Silas's favor now.

When the gunman's attention was turned toward the front desk attendants he continued to scream at, Silas moved to hide behind the concierge desk.

One of the women on the floor in the center of the lobby spotted him. Her eyes widened at the sight of him squatting with two AKs behind the desk. He hoped the fact he was in a damn business suit and was hiding from the bad guys gave her a clue he wasn't with them.

Just in case it wasn't clear he was one of the good guys, he pressed one finger to his lips. Then held up the lanyard holding the name badge he'd almost forgotten Chavez had given him at breakfast. It clearly identified him as a summit attendee.

The small tip of her head as she held eye contact with him was a good sign.

He turned his attention back to the gunman, still facing the other way and loudly repeating something he could only understand parts of.

When the man turned slightly Silas realized what he was doing. He was shouting into a radio.

That explained his panic. He couldn't get his two partners in the ballroom to respond.

*Yeah, buddy. You're right. You are completely alone here.*

They already had taken one attacker alive who could answer their questions.

From what Silas could tell in the ballroom from the location of the wound he'd inflicted and the amount of blood, the injury most likely wasn't life threatening. The bullet had missed the attacker's vest and clipped him just beneath it in his side.

If Silas was correct and the guy upstairs lived to tell his tale, that meant he didn't need to take this gunman alive.

That worked in his favor, but not much else did.

There were at least a dozen civilians down on their knees on the marble floor. Both hotel employees and guests, judging by the looks of them.

The gunman, though obviously not prepared for this attack emotionally, was well equipped for it. He, like his partners upstairs, wore a bulletproof vest.

The lobby was bright as day as the sun glared through the glass front wall. Darkness was a SEAL's best friend, but Silas was going to have to come out into the light and take out this target.

He would just have to make it work. He tuned out the fire alarm that continued to blare and zeroed in on the lone target.

When one of the hostages dared to speak, the gunman got more agitated. He raised his gun above his head and started shooting the ceiling. That accomplished two things—the hostages flattened lower to the floor and the shooter exposed his side beneath his arm where the vest didn't cover.

Weapon up, Silas took the shot. Three rounds, quick and in succession. Judging by the way the attacker reeled backward, an expression of shock on his face, at least one bullet had found its mark.

The gunman stumbled back a step and slid down the front desk to slump on the floor.

Now might be the most dangerous part of Silas's day. He was the only one upright and armed.

With an untold number of local officials outside, hyped up and ready to shoot anyone they could find, he was the only target.

But this third gunman might not be the last one. What if there were more accomplices, lying low, hidden amid the staff and guests?

Silas rolled back behind the shelter of the concierge desk and took a breath. He let seconds tick by, waiting for another bad guy to reveal himself. None did.

When the lobby hostages began to rise from the floor he knew it was decision time and he had only seconds to make his. Those front doors would be breached any second.

His gut told him this was it. It was over. There were only three. It also told him if he stood up with two AKs on him he'd be a dead man.

He put the two weapons down, sliding them far under the desk. He shoved his backpack—military grade and color—underneath too. He needed to look like a businessman, not a fighter, when he stood and revealed himself.

Once the chaos settled and the interviews with the authorities began, he'd tell the officials the location of the weapons and retrieve his backpack, which at this point didn't have a whole lot in it anyway.

He was grateful now for the suit and name badge and impractical leather shoes, since in the eyes of the men storming the lobby his appearance was that of an innocent man unconnected with the attack.

The officials were running toward the building, yelling for everyone to put their hands in the air in what sounded like the local French-laced Arabic. Silas didn't need to understand completely to comprehend what they wanted. Neither did any of the others.

Experience told him how this would go. They'd all be marched outside. He'd be one in a long line of people. That would be just the beginning of a long day of questions and containment for all of them while they investigated the scene and every person's background.

The calm after the storm would be almost unbearable with the rush of adrenaline still surging through him.

They'd eventually find out it was him who took out the attackers. Then they'd drag him into interrogation. He'd answer their many questions, many times, and try to explain how it all went down and how he happened to be able to take out three armed gunmen.

That story should keep him in custody for another eight hours or so since he was a civilian.

His first civilian kill. Two actually. And on

foreign soil. Oh yeah. That should go over real well with the local authorities.

He'd be lucky if he didn't find himself in a cell for a few hours, if not overnight.

Hopefully Chavez, or someone higher at DHS, would vouch for him. Intervene and get him out of interrogation earlier rather than later.

Meanwhile, all he wanted to do was call Maggie. He'd managed to keep his mind on the task while in the heat of battle, but now it was over his hand itched to reach for his cell phone.

He restrained the impulse for now. But damn, when he saw that woman again, he was going to kiss her until they were both breathless.

Then he was going to woo her.

Dates. Flowers. Love notes. Hopefully more sex.

Anything and everything he could do to get her back in his life, because today had been too real of a reminder that he didn't want to live in a world without her in it.

He wanted her to be his again. Completely. Not for one night. Not as friends or even friends with benefits. He wanted his wife back. He was going to marry that woman—again—if it was the last thing he did.

The authorities were still hovering outside the entrance, as if they were afraid to come inside in case there were more gunmen.

Fuck it. Silas wasn't going to wait around for them to come get him. He wasn't in the teams anymore. He could make his own damn rules.

Leaving the weapons where they were, stashed beneath the concierge desk, Silas grabbed his bag and slid backward across the hard floor of the lobby and around the corner.

Once out of sight, he scrambled to his feet and took off for the door to the stairwell. He made it without being seen and ran up the stairs, taking them two at a time.

On the second floor he stopped outside the ballroom door. Through the large crack between the two main doors he saw the summit attendees, some seated, some standing. And he saw the two men he'd left in charge standing on alert. All seemed well.

Pressed against the wall—he had no intention of falling to friendly fire—he pressed his hand against one door and shouted, "It's Silas Branson. It's safe. I'm opening the door and coming in."

When he looked again, he saw the two bodyguards facing the door but not aiming weapons at him. That was a good sign.

He saw something else too as he opened the door fully and took a step into the room—Maggie running toward him.

She hit him like a linebacker. He smiled as she threw her arms around his neck and jumped into his arms, wrapping her legs around him.

He held her tight, burying his face in her hair as she sobbed against him.

Finally, he got his head on straight and Maggie's feet back on solid ground.

"You all right?" Silas asked her.

"Yes." She drew in a shaky breath and looked at him through tear-filled eyes. "Are you?"

"Perfect," he smiled. He pulled her against him again just as Chavez walked up next to him.

"What happened downstairs?" Chavez asked.

Not wanting to get into specifics with Maggie still so shaken, he said, "Let's just say there's one less bad guy in the world."

Chavez nodded. "Good job."

"Thanks, boss."

Chavez laughed. "You keep this up, you'll be the boss soon."

Silas blew out a loud breath. "Don't worry. I don't want your job."

But there were plenty of things he did want. Maggie was at the top of his list.

What he wanted besides her was reliable and adequate security for any American delegations traveling anywhere outside of the US.

What had happened today was unacceptable and he intended to do something about it, now, while he was the hero of the moment and when he had the attention of those up the chain of command.

It was the perfect time to make his demands . . . and he knew right where to start.

# CHAPTER SEVENTEEN

Unhappily dressed in a suit once again, Silas stood when he saw the two men he was scheduled to meet walk through the door of the D.C. restaurant.

They were wearing tactical pants and short sleeved collared shirts, making him wish he'd given in to the temptation to dress down this morning. He was meeting with two SEALs who'd left the Navy and become security contractors. He should have known PMCs wouldn't be in suits.

"Thank you for meeting with me," he said when they arrived at the table.

"Of course. We'll always make time to meet with a fellow frogman," the man he knew as Jon Rudnick grinned.

Jon's partner, Zane, extended his hand. "It's good to finally get to sit down and talk to someone at DHS who doesn't have their head up their ass."

"No offense," Jon added, shooting Zane a glance.

Silas laughed. "None taken. A year later I'm still amazed I'm working there myself."

Zane bobbed his head to the side. "Well, I'm pretty confident when I say it's good for everyone that you are there."

Silently, Silas had to agree.

"So, I was surprised to hear you left the teams. I figured you'd be there at least twenty," Jon said.

"Yeah. Me too. But I blew out my back so I'm now among the civilian ranks. Medically retired."

Jon hissed in a breath between his teeth. "Jeez. I'm sorry. That's tough. Same thing happened to Rick Mann. You probably remember him. But it was his knees. Sucks being forced out if you're not ready for it."

"Yeah, it does." Silas agreed.

"But hey, we could use someone with your experience at our company. We handle mostly private security jobs. Some government contracts. Something to think about if you're looking for more action than you're getting riding a desk at DHS." Jon smiled.

Silas laughed. "Thanks. I'll keep that in mind."

A year ago he might have jumped at the chance to work for them.

Now, things had changed. That first night he'd

spent with Maggie in Chad, and the nights they'd been together since then, were certainly part of his change in attitude.

The reason for this meeting was another.

He had plans to improve how things were done at his agency to make sure what happened in Chad could never happen again.

Silas knew Jon Rudnick and Zane Alexander both by reputation and from them crossing paths on the occasional mission. And he knew of the reputation of their company, Guardian Angel Protection Services.

These two men were experts in putting military training and tactics into practice in the civilian world. That was exactly what Silas needed.

"So as I said when I called, this is really just a fact finding mission," Silas began.

Zane nodded. "Understood. We're ready for your questions."

"And if it turns out GAPS isn't a good fit for your needs, we're happy to help you brainstorm another solution," Jon said. "Half of our jobs are consultations. Though we're ready and able to provide you with manpower if that's what you need."

"I know what I want and I know what DHS needs. The problem is I'm not sure I can get them to agree. Even if they do, there's the red tape to get through to make it happen."

Jon snorted out a laugh. "Preaching to the

choir."

Zane nodded. "It's why we left. We were tired of seeing what needed to be done but wasn't. Tired of fighting the system."

Silas knew these would be the guys to speak to. They'd been there where he'd been. They'd taken their frustration and done something with it.

The waiter arrived to take their orders. After their drinks had been delivered and while they waited for their meals, Silas launched into a shortened account of what had happened in Chad. How the inadequate security at the summit had left them open for attack.

Jon shook his head. "After Libya, why is our government still trusting locals to provide security?"

Zane blew out a breath. "Apparently they've learned nothing from past mistakes."

Silas had thought the same. He nodded. "I agree. So, anyway, they're happy with me right now. After Chad, I'm on the radar of the DHS Secretary so I think this is a good time to lobby for better security for any department events or travel abroad—security that we at DHS are in control of hiring, provided by people we know, who we choose."

Zane shook his head. "They were lucky you were there. Things might have worked out completely differently if you hadn't been."

"They were damn lucky." Leaning back in his chair, Jon folded his arms. "You know, I always thought it was a waste. The government spends a fortune grooming every one of us. Making us the best of the best, and then when we leave service, years of real world experience and training goes unused. I mean we started our company, but think of the hundreds of SEALs who are out there doing . . . whatever. Not using their training, most likely."

It was like a light bulb switched on in Silas's brain.

Jon was right but it didn't have to be like that. Why should all that training and experience go to waste?

Sure, he'd found more than a few silver hairs around his temple, which he'd promptly cussed, plucked and flushed, but Silas wasn't ready to be put out to pasture just yet. What he'd accomplished in Chad with no backup and few tools was proof of that.

And he knew other officers in the same position. Good leaders who Uncle Sam had spent a fortune to train. He'd bet there were plenty who weren't ready to retire yet either. They still had too much left to give.

Jon had gone the private security route, filling his ranks with former operators, taking advantage of their skills. Why couldn't Silas do the same but within DHS?

And why stop at security for traveling DHS delegations?

What if DHS had an internal team to handle anything that came up? He was the one who got the intel about all the possible problems in the world. Instead of just collecting information and then issuing alerts, what if he could send a team to fix the problem—or avoid it in the first place?

As a lieutenant commander he'd proven he could lead a team but also work alone. There were others just like him. Retired SEAL leaders who could jump into any assignment and lead a team or work solo if necessary.

"You okay?"

At that question, Silas came back to the present. He found Jon's hand on his arm and a concerned expression on his face.

His mind was spinning. Racing so fast he realized he'd dropped the ball on all conversation and his glass was in his hand but he'd forgotten to drink.

"Yeah. I'm good." In fact, he hadn't felt this excited about something in a very long time. He smiled, almost giddy. "I'm real good."

An hour later Silas left the restaurant and the meeting with a clear idea of what he wanted. He went directly to his boss's office.

After two short knocks on the open door, he said, "Rich. Can I speak with you?"

As the Director of the Office of Operations Coordination, Richard Chavez should be the man who could put this new plan into action. And, as Silas's boss, he was the one man Silas knew well enough at DHS to present what might possibly be a crazy plan.

"Of course, Si. I've always got time for you. Have a seat."

"Thank you."

"How are you?"

"Good—" Silas began to deliver his usual rote answer and stopped. "Actually, I've been doing a lot of thinking. About Chad."

"Please tell me you're not leaving us because of what happened."

Silas glanced up to see Chavez's concern in his expression. "No, sir. No plans to quit."

At least not yet. Perhaps he'd have to reevaluate that based on how this meeting went.

Could he sit back and watch the department do the same things it had always done when he knew there was a better way? Although, could he leave knowing that if he stayed he might possibly be able to make a change?

Now was not the time for this internal debate. Now was the time to sell his plan.

"I have an idea," he said.

"All right." Chavez steepled his fingers in front of him.

"The Navy invests an enormous amount of dollars in every one of us who serve in the SEALs. The training I received in all fields as a lieutenant commander was top notch."

Chavez nodded. "Which is exactly why I hired you."

"Yes. But why stop at me?" Silas asked.

"I'm not sure what you mean. I can assure you if there is an opening in another department we'll always consider veterans to fill it, but we only need one deputy director and that's you."

"That's the thing, though. Having me, with my skills and qualifications, coordinating information—" Silas shook his head. "Our office, DHS, the country, would be better served if I was coordinating a team of men instead."

Chavez frowned. "I'm not sure what you're suggesting. Who would this team be? And what would they be doing?"

Silas leaned forward to explain. "When we access information and see a threat or a problem, what if we didn't depend on other organizations to handle it? What if we kept it all in house and dealt with situations with a DHS division staffed by former Navy commanders like me."

Chavez shook his head. "We're the Department of Homeland Security. We're not set up to run our own platoon of SEALs. That's what the Department of Defense is for."

"I'm not asking for a platoon. Just a small number of retired SEAL officers we can call on when needed who can lead a mission of multi-agency operatives." Silas lifted one shoulder. "Start small with let's say a dozen and see how it goes."

The man pressed his lips together and remained silent. Silas could only hope it was because he was considering the idea.

Finally, Chavez said, "Something like this isn't

going to have a line in our budget."

Money was one thing politicians loved to talk about—or rather complain about and use as an excuse for inaction.

From what Silas could see there was plenty of it to go around. It usually was just funneled to the wrong places. But this—the money—could be what would sink Silas's plan, even with Chavez's support for the idea.

"I understand." Silas braced himself for disappointment.

"But," Chavez continued. "There is some wiggle room in some of the budget lines for *unspecified* spending."

His hopes rose. "Yes, sir."

Chavez met his gaze. "The whole idea's a bit unorthodox. It's probably going to cause waves. We'll be accused of overstepping."

"Then don't make it public. It can be a secret division," Silas joked and then began to seriously consider the merits of the idea.

Chavez lifted a brow. "That's a good plan actually. So you do realize, I can't make a decision like this on the spot."

"I understand. And thank you for hearing me out."

"Of course. Only a fool wouldn't listen to the man who, unarmed, took out three terrorists single handedly." Chavez grinned.

"I wasn't unarmed. I had a knife and a pack of

matches." Silas laughed.

Chuckling, Chavez shook his head. "Go home, Si. Enjoy your weekend."

"Thanks. See you Monday." Hopefully, he'd have an answer by then, but he wasn't going to plan on it. Something like this could drag out for months, or more, but at least he'd gotten the ball rolling.

Resolved, Silas was happy to put work on the back burner and look forward to the next three blissful nights with Maggie.

He hadn't even made it to her place in Virginia Beach yet when his cell vibrated with a text.

Silas glanced at the display and saw it was from Chavez.

He pulled over onto the shoulder and opened the text.

*I crunched the numbers. We can swing it. You've got your secret division. Better come up with a name for it. You'll be heading up this thing.*

Chavez had found the budget for it. *Holy shit.*

Alone in the truck he resisted the urge to whoop for joy.

As far as the name, Silas had that covered. Having lunch with Zane and Jon and talking about stories from the old days back in BUD/S and their years in the teams had given him the idea for a name. A symbol that unofficially represented the SEALs.

He typed it into the text. *Bone Frog Command.*

The bone frog had been tattooed on Navy SEALs for decades. It seemed fitting it would represent this new DHS secret division that would give former frogmen like himself a second life.

His division, his idea, was about to come to life.

It was a sweet victory worth celebrating.

It was Friday and, even though a year ago he'd told Chavez he wouldn't be doing the D.C. to Virginia Beach commute every weekend, he'd been doing it lately—happily.

He couldn't get home fast enough that evening.

*Home.*

Okay. Not exactly. It was still Maggie's home and he was just a visitor, but in the three weeks since they'd gotten home from Chad he'd spent more than a few nights there. He was happy to spend every second he could get with her. He was more than tired of living like a bachelor.

He was good at being married. They were good together. And tonight he got to not only see Maggie after five long days of being away from her while he was in D.C., but he also had the new Bone Frog Command to celebrate.

He'd have to decide what he could and couldn't tell her about his new secret division, but he'd figure it out. As a SEAL's wife she'd kept his secrets before. She'd keep this one too, but all that would come in time.

The euphoria of the day, from the meeting with Jon and Zane, to the text from Chavez, had Silas pulling into a shopping center on a whim.

He'd spotted the jewelers sign and couldn't

resist just looking.

It didn't hurt to see what they had. Maybe pick Maggie up a trinket. Earrings or whatever.

Just because he walked right over and was looking at the diamond rings didn't mean he was going to buy one.

"Can I help you?" the salesman asked.

"Just looking, thanks."

"Of course. Take your time."

"Actually." Silas pointed to one. "Can I see that one?"

"The pink diamond pave?" the salesman asked.

"Um, yeah." He didn't know what the hell *pave* was but the ring he had his eye on had pink diamonds—and Maggie would love it.

He held the small band between his two fingers and remembered buying that first ring for her years ago. He'd known then just as he knew now, he wanted to live and die married to this woman.

That first time he'd been nervous buying the ring and asking that question that would change the course of both their lives.

He'd been foolish for feeling unsure then. They'd been head over heels in love. There was no question in either of their minds they'd get married.

But so much had happened since then. His nerves as he held this ring today were justified.

That didn't stop him from thrusting it toward the clerk and saying, "I'll take it."

"Wonderful. Do you need it sized?"

"Probably." But he didn't want to wait. Now he'd made the decision, he wanted to do it tonight. "Any chance it's a six?"

The clerk checked the tag and smiled. "It must be fate. It is a six."

If he'd been looking for a sign, that might just be it. Fate, for once, was working in his favor.

"All right then." Silas laughed and dug his wallet out of his pocket.

He made good money now and he couldn't think of anything better to spend it on. He tossed his credit card on the glass counter and pulled out his cell.

As the clerk ran the card, Silas punched in a text.

*Be there shortly. Need anything?*

Her response came back fast and had his heart speeding.

*Just you.*

Silas blew out a breath, nerves kicking up a notch. No doubt about it. He was doing this.

Tonight he was getting down on one knee and making Maggie his again.

# CHAPTER EIGHTEEN

Maggie answered the door looking beautiful in a dress and heels.

"Wow. You look great." Silas stepped inside and leaned in for a kiss before asking, "We going out for dinner?"

She raised her gaze to him and gave a sly shake of her head. "No. We're staying in."

"Okay." He grinned.

He didn't object to his woman in a sexy dress, especially not when she looked at him like that, with heat in her eyes. She had incredible legs. And later, when the time came, that dress would provide some easy access when he sat her in his lap on the sofa when they watched a movie on TV.

Lacing her fingers through his, she pulled him toward the kitchen.

He inhaled the aroma as he walked inside. "Stroganoff?"

"Yes."

"Mmm." He peeked into the pot. "My favorite."

"I know." She poured red wine into a glass and handed it to him. "That's why I made it."

What he'd done to deserve such treatment he didn't know, but he wasn't going to question his good fortune.

"How was work?" she asked.

"Really good actually."

She raised a brow. "Really? Good. I'm glad."

"And how was your week?" he asked, mostly to change the subject to try and keep himself from spilling the beans to her about Bone Frog Command.

"Good." She pinned him with her blue gaze. "Can we be done with small talk now?"

"Sure." He nodded with a laugh. "Why? You starving? We can eat—"

She fisted the lapels of his suit, pulled him down to meet her and kissed him hard and deep.

Taken by surprise, he managed to get his wine glass planted on the table without spilling any before wrapping his arms around her back. She was hungry all right, but obviously not for food.

He could be on board with that. He stroked his

tongue against hers happy to comply with whatever she wanted.

In fact, why were they standing in the kitchen when there was a sofa just feet away? Silas hoisted her against him, carrying her to the living room before he tumbled them both onto the cushions.

He still wasn't used to being with her again after their year apart. It still felt a bit like he was a teenager about to get lucky for the first time as he hooked his fingers beneath her underwear and tugged them down her legs.

She wrestled to unfasten his shirt buttons as he moved on to his belt. They'd make it to the bed eventually tonight, but not yet. Right now, he couldn't get inside this woman fast enough.

As he flipped her onto her back and kneeled between her legs on the sofa cushion, he said, "I promise, one day I'll be able to control myself around you."

"Don't you dare," she said, grabbing his ass with both hands and pulling him toward her.

Silas groaned as he felt her wet heat tease his tip. "All right. Whatever you want."

He really did love all the many, many things they could—and had—done together but the urge to sink inside her, possess her, claim her, had ridden him strong since Chad.

Once he got that need out of his system tonight, they'd get to the other stuff. He'd make her come until she writhed against his tongue and begged him to stop. Later.

For now it was all he could do to keep his eyes open so he could watch her expression as he slid inside.

He hissed in a breath as the feel of being in her surrounded him.

One hand braced on the arm of the sofa and the other holding her hips up to give him a better angle, he stroked inside.

"I want to get married." Her words had his hand slipping off the sofa arm as he nearly face planted into the pillow behind her head.

He managed to catch himself and stared down at her in shock. "Say again?"

"I want us to get remarried."

A short laugh escaped him. This woman always could surprise him.

Still buried inside her, he obviously had some unfinished business. Since she'd just given him everything he wanted—her becoming his wife—he intended to celebrate, first by finishing what they'd started. Then by making it official with a proper proposal.

He smiled as he leaned low and pressed a brief but tender kiss to her lips. "Yeah. Okay."

She returned his smile. "Good."

Silas cocked up a brow. "Can we get back to what we were doing now?"

"Yes, please." Her heavily lidded gaze drew him forward.

Cupping her face with his palm, he kissed her while they made love.

Slow. Fast. It didn't matter. When he was with this woman she consumed him, body and soul.

He managed to hold on until he heard her breath hitch and felt her muscles tighten around him. She came, hard and loud, and he followed seconds later.

When he moved to get off her rather than stay and enjoy the aftershocks as her body gripped his, she groaned. "No. Don't get up yet."

"Give me one second, sweetie. I promise I'm coming right back." He stood and pulled on his underwear and pants.

He'd be damned if he proposed naked even if the first part of this process had begun with him inside her.

Silas pulled the small ring box out of his pocket while she struggled to sit upright.

"What's that?" she asked, her gaze moving from the deep blue velvet box in his hand to his face.

"It's what I was going to give you tonight after dinner. But you went and stole my thunder." He opened the lid.

Her eyes went wide as she looked from the ring to him.

"So, I think we've already covered this part, but humor me."

It wasn't exactly as he'd imagined. He was barefoot and his shirt was unbuttoned, but the timing still felt absolutely perfect.

Silas got down on one knee as Maggie

straightened her dress and sat on the edge of the sofa, watching, waiting.

"Maggie O'Leary Branson, will you do me the honor of becoming my wife?"

She nodded, her eyes glassy with tears. "Yes."

With the balance of power restored and his man card firmly back in his possession, Silas slipped the ring onto her finger. It slid on perfectly, as if it had been made for her. That seemed fitting, because he'd always felt she'd been made just for him.

She fingered the ring, watching the diamonds catch the light. "It's beautiful."

"You're beautiful," he said.

Wiping a tear, she glanced up at him. "I love you."

"And I love you. I always have and I always will." Even with all that happened, all the many losses and changes in his life, that had never changed.

But something had altered within him.

For the first time in a long time, he wasn't afraid to look ahead to the future and feel hope again.

# EPILOGUE

Silas had never seen anything so frightening . . . and he'd seen a lot in his life.

He ignored the tremble in his hand as he took the small white plastic stick from his wife. She was smiling as she handed it to him.

Now the reason for her unannounced visit to his office in the middle of a workday made sense.

Why was she smiling when the sight struck cold hard fear in his heart?

One word, spelled out in tiny blue letters to fit inside the area that displayed the test results, was enough to have his knees weak.

Pregnant.

He raised his gaze to meet hers. "What does this mean?"

A frown drew her brows low over her sky blue eyes. "What do you mean, what does it mean? I'm pregnant."

Yeah, he got that.

Hard to miss when it was right there in black and white. Or rather blue and white. But what did it mean to her? To him? To their life together?

He swallowed hard and handed the offending stick back to her. "Mags, we weren't planning for this."

She drew back. "What are you saying? You don't want this baby?"

"No, that's not what I'm saying. Not at all."

He obviously should have considered this possibility and been a little more careful with his swimmers.

Although in his defense, there had been a lot going on in their lives the past seven months.

Their wedding. The birth of his own baby— Bone Frog Command.

She'd been on birth control for so many years, they'd both gotten used to not having to be careful.

When the doctor suggested she should really go off the pills after so many years, she had. But he couldn't bring himself to start using condoms. This was his fault. At thirty-eight years old he was pretty set it in his ways.

But now that a baby was a reality, of course he wanted it. He just didn't want to want it.

Time for honesty, with himself and with her. "I'm scared."

"Scared of what?" she asked.

"What if something happens to him—" He stopped himself, realizing he was already connecting this baby with Jonas by assuming it was a boy. Already fearing a loss and what that would do to him.

Her expression softened. "It won't."

"It could. And what if something happens to you? We're not as young as we used to be. Things happen."

"Jeez, Si. I'm not that old. Women have babies in their late thirties and even their forties all the time."

"I know." It wasn't just age he was worried about.

"You're thinking about Jonas." She laid one hand on his arm.

He let out a short bitter laugh. "Of course, I am." He'd never stop thinking about Jonas.

Maggie shook her head. "It's not going to happen again."

"Just because I'm retired and stateside now?" He hated the harsh tone he heard in his voice. He met her gaze and said, "Sorry."

She shook her head. "No, don't apologize. I understand what you're feeling, but it'll be okay."

He reached out and drew her against him, hugging her tight. Having her close quieted his racing pulse. "A baby. Wow."

Of all the many changes in his life, that was the one thing he hadn't even considered.

She laughed against his chest before she leaned back to look up at him. "Don't worry. You have some time to get used to the idea."

Good, because he was going to need it. But even during the last few minutes since she'd told him, the idea had begun to settle in.

He was calmer as the first wave of panic subsided. And now that he was no longer paralyzed by terror, the last place he wanted to be was at the office.

"Let's go out and celebrate," he said.

She frowned. "Don't you have to work?"

Crap. There was that.

Bone Frog Command had added a huge workload to his job. And it wasn't anything he could hand off to anyone else.

He remembered he had a meeting in—he glanced at the time on his watch—five minutes.

Double crap. Celebrating was going to have to wait.

He blew out a breath. "All right. How about this? I wrap up some things here at work and I'll meet you at home. Then we can decide where to go for an early dinner. We could make reservations at that new Italian place in Alexandria you've been wanting to try."

She'd transferred to the D.C. office right before the wedding and they'd made a new home and a new life together—a good life—there in Washington.

No more commuting on weekends. He fell to sleep and woke next to her every day, as it should be.

"Or . . ." Maggie's expression turned sultry, almost devilish. She ran one manicured nail down the front of his shirt. "You could pick up take-out on the way home and we could stay in."

He laughed, easily grasping the meaning of her not so subtle hint.

His wife obviously wanted to celebrate in a more private way and, still a little shell shocked by her news or not, he was completely up for that plan.

"Yeah, we can definitely do that." He released his hold on her, but only after pressing a much too brief kiss to her lips. "Unfortunately, I've got a meeting to get to now."

"I'll let you go. I wanted to stop in Victoria's Secret anyway."

That meant tonight he'd be treated to a viewing of Maggie in her new lingerie.

He shook his head as his cock reacted to that image. "Jesus, woman. How am I supposed to concentrate in that meeting now?"

She tossed the pregnancy test into the trashcan by the door before she sent him a steamy glance as she reached for the doorknob. "You'll figure it out.

See you later. Love you."

"Love you." He watched her go and then had to wrestle his attention back to what he was supposed to be doing.

What had that been again? Right. The meeting.

He moved toward the door, trying to pull himself out of his newlywed mindset and get back into lieutenant commander mode.

As he reached for the knob, his gaze landed on the trashcan. He stopped short, his hand resting on the knob but he didn't open the door. It was as if he'd forgotten what he'd been about to do.

The pregnancy test sat innocently on top of a Styrofoam take-out container. Just a little piece of plastic, but it had the power to rattle him. Him, a battle hardened SEAL commander.

He blew out a breath and actually managed to get the door open this time.

He had two minutes to compose himself as he made his way from his office to that of the Deputy Secretary of the Department of Homeland Security.

Inside the meeting room, more people than he'd expected to see sat at the table. And not lower level staffers either, but agency heads.

He lifted a brow. If the heavy hitters were in attendance something big was up. Though he should have realized that even before entering the room, simply from the fact he'd only been given thirty minutes notice for this emergency meeting.

Something had happened. The only question

was, what?

That was apparently soon to be answered. The representative from the Secret Service glanced up and cleared his throat.

Looking concerned, he said, "Sorrel is missing."

Silas's eyes popped wide at hearing the code name the Secret Service used for the first daughter.

What the fuck? It couldn't be. The President's teenage wild child daughter was missing?

Holy shit.

"Evidence suggests she's been in communication with a certain cult leader's son. It's feared she's run off with him. If that is the case, of course POTUS wants this issue resolved as quickly and as quietly as possible."

Which would make it the perfect job for Bone Frog Command. In fact, Silas had the perfect man in mind for the job—Garrett Tierney.

Silas voiced as much. "My division can handle this. Quick and quiet."

The Deputy Secretary nodded. "I agree. Get on it right away. Keep me updated, but I'll trust you and your team to handle this."

Just the way he liked it.

"Yes, ma'am." Silas stood, the adrenaline pumping as he took the folder the secret service handed him. "I'll go make the call."

Time to save the day. Now, in light of what Maggie had shared, he had more reason than ever to make sure he and his team were there to rid the world of everything bad in it. Bring it on!

Dear Reader,

I hope you liked Silas's story and reading about how Bone Frog Command was born.

The stories of the men of Bone Frog continue in SEAL Love's Legacy by Sharon Hamilton with Navy SEAL commander Garrett Tierney.

And if you enjoyed meeting Jon Rudnick and Zane Alexander from GAPS, you can read their stories, and those of their SEAL friends, in my Hot SEALs series.

As always, happy reading!

XOXO
*Cat*

# SILVER SEALS

SEAL Strong – Cat Johnson
SEAL Love's Legacy – Sharon Hamilton
SEAL Together – Maryann Jordan
SEAL of Fortune – Becky McGraw
SEAL in Charge – Donna Michaels
SEAL in a Storm – KaLyn Cooper
SEAL Forever – Kris Michaels
SEAL Out of Water– Abbie Zanders
Sign, SEAL and Deliver – Geri Foster
SEAL Hard – J.M. Madden
SEAL Undercover – Desiree Holt
SEAL for Hire – Trish Loye
SEAL at Sunrise – Caitlyn O'Leary

SilverSEALs.com

*Don't miss Cat Johnson's*
Hot SEALs

Night with a SEAL
Saved by a SEAL
SEALed at Midnight
Kissed by a SEAL
Protected by a SEAL
Loved by a SEAL
Tempted by a SEAL
Wed to a SEAL
Romanced by a SEAL
Rescued by a Hot SEAL
Betting on a Hot SEAL
Escape with a Hot SEAL
Matched with a Hot SEAL
SEAL the Deal
Hot SEAL in Hollywood

CatJohnson.net

# ABOUT THE AUTHOR

Cat Johnson is a top 10 *New York Times* bestseller and the author of the *USA Today* bestselling Hot SEALs series. She writes contemporary romance featuring sexy alpha heroes and is known for her unique marketing. She has sponsored pro bull riders, owns a collection of camouflage and western wear for book signings, and has used bologna to promote romance novels.

Never miss a new release or a deal again. Join Cat's inner circle at catjohnson.net/news for email alerts.

22611323R00107

Made in the USA
San Bernardino, CA
15 January 2019